Living Among the Believers
Stories from the Holy Land down the Ganges

Sachi G. Dastidar

To
Amitabha & Lisa
Congratulation !
Sachi G. Dastidar
and
Dastidar Family
July 18, 2009

FIRMA KLM PRIVATE LIMITED
KOLKATA   *   *   *   2006

Published by :
FIRMA KLM PRIVATE LIMITED
257-B, B. B. Ganguly Street,
Kolkata – 700 012
INDIA
E-mail : firmaklm@yahoo.com
Website : www.firmaklm.net

First Published : Mahalaya 22 Sept. 2006, Kolkata (Calcutta)

© Author

ISBN   81-7102-140-9

Cover Design : Partha Sarkar
Photographs by Author

Composed by :
Desktop Printers
5/2, Garstin Place
Kolkata-700 001

Printed by :
Unik Print & Process
61A, Keshab Sen Street,
Kolkata - 700 009

To my friends

Jill Hamberg
Jay Hyman
Chitta Ranjan Mazumder
Mohsin Siddique
Arlene Wilhelm

CONTENTS

PREFACE

These are stories about the effects of another 9/11 that took place almost a century ago and its aftermath a century later in a different continent. Stories are about the victims of that violent act but yet unknown to the hunmanity. That 9/11 took place in the Indian Province of Bengal in Colonial India on 10/16, October 16, 1905, at the instigation of then British Administration. Imperial Britain partitioned Bengal in to Muslim East Bengal and secular non-Muslim West Bengal Provinces within British India starting the process of intolerant, communal (racist) and extremist groups to rise to power in Muslim-majority East Bengal, now Bangladesh, and in the Muslim-majority provinces of Colonial Northwest India and Punjab, now Pakistan. That divisive process brought the Muslim-non Muslim partition of India in 1947 and the eventual rise of extremist Islamism in Pakistan (and in neighboring Afghanistan) and Bangladesh and an extremist Communist Party-Marxist to power in West Bengal. But what happened to the indigenous peoples in the Islamized area who did not yet convert to monotheistic faiths, or, those who could not flee to new India? And what happened to those who fled to India? Colonial British rulers wanted to check the aspirations of Indians to be free — of all faiths, ethnicities and linguistic groups — but unleashed a force that they did not and could not control, almost paralleling American and Western support for anti-Soviet Taliban in Afghanistan 90 years later, and then the rise of intolerant bin-Laden and finally 9/11. Under pressure from the pan-Indian nationalists, that 1905 partition was annulled in 1911 and the province was reunited in 1912, but that process of communal divide created a permanent India-Pakistan partition in 1947 and a precarious life for many of its own citizens. How precarious?

In the Subcontinent Bengalis were known to other Indians for scholarly discourses and leadership in literature, philosophy, religion, nationalism, history, education, arts, music and science. But those discourses and leadership stopped with the second 1947 Partition of Bengal in the middle of 20th century when the Bengali Hindu culture took a turn toward atheism away from nationalism, rationalism, spirituality and philosophy and Muslim Bengali towards Arabized Islamism. If the first partition of 1905 produced flowering of literature and litterateur including the national anthems of both India and Bangladesh, the much severe 1947 partition provided the death nail to the 6th largest linguistic group of the world, and no introspection. With that came stillness in writing and scholarly work on Partition, about their own persecuted families, even when a large state like West Bengal (2001 population 75 million) containing between 25 to 30 million Bangadeshi refugee and their off-spring, or Tripura (3 million) with 2/3 being Bangladeshi Hindu refugee and their descendents.

Breaking a taboo, one of my essays, *Ai Bangla, Oi Bangla* (This Bengal, That Bengal) was published in *Desh* in August of 1989 the largest circulation Bengali/Indian weekly with debates on the article raging for over six months in Bangladesh and in India. A Bengali book by the same name was published in 1992 (College Street Publication, Calcutta) which was reviewed and/or discussed by all the major newspapers and journals in West Bengal and Bangladesh. In 1998 a collection of my Bengali short stories was published in *A Aamar Desh* (This is my home, Tulat Publishers, Calcutta). In between a number of Bengali short fictions were published from early 1990s to early 2000s, but mostly in Bengali. Those appeared in weeklies, monthlies, fortnightly journals and special issues published from New York, West Bengal (India) and Bangladesh. For a long time special literary journals have been an unique feature of Bengali culture and they appear during

Durga Puja, Saraswati Puja, *Nababarsha* (New Year), *Ekushey* (21st February), Id (Muslim festival) and Tagore's Birthday celebrations and more. To my great surprise, all of my fictions were reprinted one of more times at various journals. At least one, *'Nivaranir swargabash'* (Nivarani goes to heaven) was reprinted, to my knowledge, five times in five different publications in New York, India and Bangladesh. Once I was pleasantly surprised when I accidentally found during my visit to the Subcontinent that one of my articles in a Durga Puja journal published from a remote Munshiganj district in Bangladesh where I did not yet set my foot. My books and articles in English covered a wide variety of areas from housing to country hopping, and from economics to politics.

The idea of this book developed as sections of many of my Bengali short fictions were translated from time-to-time for non-native individuals. These stories revolve around the effects of one of that major event of 20th century: the Partition of India into a pluralistic, secular India and an Islamic Pakistan and Islamized Bangladesh. Independenc of Pakistan and Bangladesh have been associated with ethnic cleansing of non-Muslims, attack on their own native, indigenous, pre-Islamic cultures and institutions. It also revolves around one of the major yet unknown facts about Islamized Bangladesh: the loss of over 30 million, with descendants 45 million, Hindus from the land including over 3 million killed, and subsequent effects of that loss on non-Muslim minorities, their homes, their aspirations, their identity and Bangladesh's indigenous festivals, religion and on the pro-tolerant majority Muslims. In November 2003, I presented my findings at their invitation: Where Do My People Go; Quest of Bangladeshi Hindu Minorities, at the Holocaust and Genocide Panel of the *Annual Meetings of the American Academy of Religion* in Atlanta, Georgia. Some of these stories also revolve around the poor and oppressed co-religionists that the elite Hindu *Bhadralok*, gentlemen, left behind for safety of India but never cared to look back at the people who protected them earlier.

Although two states of India, West Bengal and Tripura, are run by Bangladeshi Hindu refugees – locally known as *Bangals* or East Bengalis — yet it has been a taboo in that fatalistic Hindu society to discuss their families they left behind; the sister lost, brother killed, mother raped, father crippled, temples destroyed and homes torched. This has been true not only for the ruling atheist Communist Party-Marxist governments in both the Bengali-speaking states but also of the former nationalist Congress Party governments run by believers, or for pro-Hindu groups. No elite in right mind wants to weaken their ruling status in India by expressing the truth, as sad as that might be. On the other hand, during our visits to remote villages what has been heartening to my family and me is that amidst the desperation of the neglected victims is the warmth that we have received from all corners of the society. Muslim and Hindu accepted us as one with whom they could express their joy and sorrow. Having my wife wearing sari and traditional Hindu symbols of married woman like the villagers themselves and having children on our journeys were big help. Doors opened easily to women, especially by other women and to a family traveling with kids. I was always invited to intimate quarters in family's home without any hesitation. Women broke traditional barriers by hugging a stranger male, like their own family members, to welcome into their families. As visits by people whose families have fled to India to escape Islamic persecution are so rare that during one of our visits a sufferer woman read in an emotion-filled voice:

Welcome

Warm hearted welcome

Greetings to the travelers,

Drifting powerless we are,
Yet in your gift, we forget our helplessness.
To grow up, to survive
Your sacrifice for us
We do not fail to remember.
Your gift 'n affection,
Heartily we can take assurance to live.
We forget once again, we've no one
But only you.
Father's affection, mother's caress, sister's love
You're giving.
So, why should we feel weak?
No, no, no, we're none of that
'Cause of your gift and sacrifice make us forget
Love of our father, mother, sister.
You're here, nothing can we give
Only our warm welcome from our warm hearts
We want to fill your heart,
And we want to seek from you,
Our claim to live.
'Gave us, you'll give, you'll take us as your own,
Please accept our salutation, Oh dear traveler,
This is our humble prayer.

Indeed vast number of non-Muslim minorities in Bangladesh,
mostly poor belonging to the traditionally oppressed Hindu castes,
live truly a precarious life. My stories are based on their lives,
stories narrated to me. They were written between 1990 and

2005. For reasons of personal safety, some names of individuals and their village names have been changed as I have no power to protect them from the thugs. Many of the articles are inspired either by my Bengali stories or reports in English that I have written for journals and newspapers.

This book would not have been possible without the encouragement of my dear friend Tapan Kumar Das. I thank Srimati Swathi Mukherji, the publisher, for taking up the project. I was helped a lot by Kashinath Pal for taking time to read the manuscript. Special thanks are due to our son Shuvo and daughter Joyeeta for being willing travelers to all corners of the Indian Subcontinent; and my wife Shefali for being a patient companion at home and abroad.

Sachi (Sabyasachi) Ghosh Dastidar
New York
October 16, 2005
Centenary of Bengal Partition.

Chapter 1

Nivarani Goes to Heaven

Whenever we set foot at Gauripur village, Nivarani would come running towards us, many others would follow her as well. In terms of connection through our souls, I was Niva's uncle, or *kaka*, although the term *kaka* would mean according to village custom, a respectful address rather than an aged or blood-related person. My children used to call Niva as *Niva-masi*, Aunt Niva. Whenever we would arrive there they would be at a loss as to how to help us. As soon we arrived, they'd offer us *daab*, the green cocoanut, for us to drink its milk. If plucked hard cocoanut was available at home, they would treat us with its cocoanut-meat. They would ask the kids to climb tall *chalta* trees and fetch the geen sour *chalta* fruit. Nivas are very poor. Year round they do not have two square meals a day. But in the village they were our only support, and yet unknown to us how we became their hope. In our visits to the village we were able to keep our valuable luggage safely at their home and visit other places. Besides, outside their home the space called 'toilet' with partial covering of bamboo *darma* net was of great help, especially to the ladies.

Gauripur is like any other non-descript, yet picturesque evergreen village of Indian Subcontinent where most people eke out a living depending on the fruits of that fertile land. Residents take a special pride in the name of Gauripur — the land (*pur*) of Mother Goddess Gauri, one of 108 names of Goddess Durga, the killer of Demons, and wife of Lord Shiva, the God of Compassion. It is said that the daughters of the village grow up with qualities like Ma Gauri — fearlessness, strong, caring, protector of her children. Last year some of Gauripur's neighbors proposed to Islamize the village by changing her 'Hindu' name to Gazipur, much as the district of Joydebpur named after one of the pre-Islamic Bengali poet Joydeb was changed to Gazipur by Arabizing the name.

Before any visit to my *desh* home, I always used to write Niva and her parents. This time too I wrote to them (I am) "coming to Dhaka on this date. But I am afraid I cannot go to my village this time. Time is too short. I must visit a lot of places on this trip. I would stay either at Naserda's house or at Bibhutida's ....." the homes of 'older brothers' Naser, a Muslim or Bhibhuti, a Hindu.

As soon as I reached Dhaka, I was informed that someone from the village came to see me, and he said it was very urgent. He would come again tomorrow at sunrise. I could not think who that could be. One needs a lot of money and time to come to Dhaka. The journey involves bus, rickshaw, steamer and walking. It is a lot of money for those whom I know!

Before I woke up from my sleep, the servant boy of the house called for me. "Sir, somebody is calling you." I organized myself and came downstairs. It was a man wearing a *lungi*, the sarong-like men's wrap, and a shirt. Before I could speak he saluted me *aadab* in Muslim and *namaskar* in Hindu styles, then quickly bend down to touch my feet to offer *pranam* greetings. I resisted him touching my feet and caught hold of his hands offering my *namaskar* greeting and said, "Please don't mind, I still cannot recognize you." The man smiled and replied with his hands folded, "Can't you remember Uncle *(Kaka)*? I am Ramjan (a Muslim). I am coming from Gauripur village. Niva's parents have sent me. On your last visit I came with you to the neighboring Durgapur village. For some time I carried your hand bag. you sent back some photos and gave us money to buy sweets."

"Yes, yes, now I remember. Isn't your daughter's name is Radha" (lord Sri Krishna's lady-love, a Hindu sage)? "So, *Ramjanbabu*, Mr. Ramjan, why have you come such a long way? When did you arrive? Where are you staying?"

"Why are you calling me *babu* or *saheb* (mister), "the formal invocation for Hindu or Muslim gentleman?" I am a peasant. I am staying with one of my *fufa* paternal cousins in a slum that side. Came day-before-yesterday. Aunt *Kaki* told me that you will give me my traveling expenses." Mr. Ramjan kept silent for sometime, thereafter gathering himself; he slowly took the name of Allah and the Prophet, and muttered something to himself. Then spelt out boldly "Niva is no more. She is dead. Her fifteen year old daghter would have been finished as well. A *Maulabi* Islamic preacher and several young men from the village were after her. I have heard that one of your relations, who now live in Dhaka, has saved Purnima's life. Didn't your relation tell you that? the villagers have sent me to take you to our village."

What Mr. Ramjan said I later heard from Kamalda, senior brother Kamal, as well. If I did not see it for myself, and came to know of it from the victims themselves I would not have believed it. I know security is a far cry in the villages. Then there is less security for women living in villages as well as in the cities. Then there is practically no security for the minority Hindu, Christian, Buddhist or tribal communities whether they are rich or poor. Nivarani belongs to such a village, yet quite smart and intelligent. If she had hailed from a middle-class family she could have done a lot.Nevertheless,by sheer talent Niva became the head of the '*Swayang-sampurna Graam Samiti,*' self-sufficient villge organization. Thereafter at a government program she became a '*Samaj Sebika*,' social worker. There she earned a few hundred takas (less than ten U.S. dollars.)

Lately there are two trends of oppression of minorities at home. One trend is that if the person belongs to the non-Muslim minority middle-class or educated family then the person is humiliated through the efforts of the government and semi-government agencies, police, military, para-military Ansar, politicians, bureaucrats and through opportunist intellectuals: Non-hiring into jobs, debarring or putting obstacles in job promotion, denial of police record keeping of atrocities, forcible confiscation of minority Hindu land and property through Enemy Property Act, destruction and looting of homes-temples-churches-student hostels, *smasan*-cremation grounds, etc. And for the poor, in addition to confiscating their homestead through the collusion of police, bureaucracy and politicians, there is rape and forcible conversion of their minor girls, and rape of wives and motherly persons. Besides, in some areas there is persecution either by the ruling parties or by the opposition. Pressures started to be exerted on both Niva and her fifteen year-old daughter Purnima by the thug '*goonda-revolutionaries*' beloging to both sides, said Mr. Ramjan. Finally, in the middle of the night Niva fled to Dhaka holding her daughter's hand. There both the mother and daughter started working in the garment industry while living on top of a swamp, finally succumbing to untimely death due to starvation and oppression. At the time of happiness and sorrow Nivas used to come rushing to Kamalda, their only protection. Many minorities today can not even say, "She is saved by death." Niva could not say that either. I've heard from many that at times even obstructions are imposed on cremation of the (Hindu-Buddhist) dead. After the death of an uncle of my friend the bereaved family was warned "Do not take the dead body of the *malaun*," a derogatory word for the lowly-filthy non-believer infidels, "at that time of the day. Do not pass through that *para* neighborhoods. Those roads are closed to dead *malauns*, etc. etc......" Even God does not know how low we have gone down while taking His name. Yet some of the sympathetic friends of the Doctor Uncle and the patients cured by him hesitated to extend a helping hand except the few fearless persons with backbone. Kamalda had to overcome great hurdles in cremating the body of Nivarani. At last with the help of the

Ramakrishna Mission the body was cremated practically by the side of a road. Now-a-days many *smasan* cremation grounds have become 'enemy' of the state as those have been confiscated by the rich and the middle-class through the bite of the Enemy Property Act. The helpless and orphaned Purnima asked her Kamaldadu, Grandpa Kamal, again and again "Won't Ma look after me from the heaven?"

For the last few minutes Ramjanbabu, Mr. Ramjan, only shed tears, and said, "I could not save Niva. You all kindly look after Purnima and the other children." Before I could finish conversation with him, Mukulbabu (Mr. Mukul), Aditya and (the Buddhist monk) *Bhantey* had already arrived, many others were to arrive the same day.

I had to accompany them for an invitation to Mukulbabu's village next day. The door was opened by a widow. Last time I saw her at the house of Mr. Bibhuti DuttaGupta. At that time, she along with her son, daughter-in-law and grandson all worked at Bidhutibabu's household. On that visit Aunt *Mashi* told me, "our house is far away, at Ganga-chhari beyond Rangpur. There I used to do some traditional handiwork." Later at an opportune time, while gossiping with aunt, I asked, "*Mashi*, what do you do when someone dies there?"

"What to do, we cremate the body!"

"Then, you must have nice cremation areas?"

"Yes." I was relieved. Mashi continued, "At our area we have many Hindu fishermen, weavers, Brahmin (priests), farmers and craftsman. There the *smasan* cremation ground is next to our *mandir* temple. All the pujas are held at that *mandir*. Even Durga Puja, the festival of 'Mother Goddess' return to Earth. But the folks of the in-law of my son face great difficulty at their place.

2

The cremation ground there is very old. Now they are not allowed to be cremated there. Those who can afford they have to send the dead bodies to a far-off place, about 30-40 miles away. Burial is also not allowed. You have no choice but to do *mukhagni*, touch the Eternal Fire on the lips, and let the dead body float down the river. Don't you see how difficult it is here?"

We talked a lot while going to Mukulbabu's village. He told me that there are many Hindu (tribal) Santhal and Christian families as well. Many people there are engaged in the traditional handspun *Khaddar* garment making. On the way he also told me that "a poor lady would come to see you . She occasionally works for us." I asked him why is she coming to see me, but he did not reply.

As I was leaving, suddenly a lady appeared and without any word touched my feet for *pranam* greetings, and placed two guavas on my hand and said in the local dialect "these are for you." She wore sari with *ghomta* hood covering her head, there was no parting of her hair, which was tightly combed backwards. Her right arm was bare (of bangles) only one *baki* iron zigzag bangle adorned her left arm. She was, perhaps, having a talk with Mukulbabu outside the house and was waiting for me. Mukul pointed to her and said, "I was talking to you about this lady. Her name is Anwara," an Arabic Muslim name. "She wanted to meet you." Looking at Anwara Mr. Mukul said, "Lakshmi, you can tell him what you wanted to say". For quite some time Mrs. Anwara looked down towards my feet, and then turned around and slowly walked away. Mukulbabu looked at Mrs. Anwara and called her and said "Where are you going Lakshmi? Why don't you call Ashok." A young man was standing at a distance; possibly around 22 to 24 years of age. "Ashok, Why don't you come here? Why are you standing at a distance?" He added "Ashok's new name is Mahboob," a Persian Muslim name.

Walking alongside Mrs. Anwara somehow uttered, "Babu, Sir, I couldn't. You please tell him. You've Ashok here."

Mrs. Anwara is a routine affair in our villages, which our intellectuals barely notice. Mrs. Anwara's real name is *Srimati* (Mrs.) Lakshmi Rani Dutta. During the Liberation War (1971) a section of her family was exterminated, including her father-in-law. Now her household included her widowed mother-in-law, two little son and daughter and her husband Anil. She was managing the household with the help of Anil's tiny street-side condiment shop and her meager income from being a part-time maid. Within a very short time there was an attack on Anil's shop. They were ordered to leave their Charan-danga home for India. It was not enough for the evictors if Nivas left for the town of Iswardi after writing them off their ancestral homestead and Anil's shop. Otherwise they would have to produce ten thousand takas immediately. Anil's mother told them "How can we get so much money? Where can we go leaving our country? This land is ours too." Before the end of the year Anil was murdered in his shop. Everybody knew who the killers were, including police. The police, village *morol* headmen and *matabbar* leading men conferred, "There's nothing that Hindus, Christians and Santhals could do. They could have given that ransom." Still, where could Lakshmi *Devi*, go? There after started mental torture by the headmen and the leading men. "What is there left of you? Why are you still living as infidel *malauns*?" Even those friends and relations who came to help them used to be insulted in filthy language. A short while later the corpse of the mother-in-law was discovered in a pond, and before the last rites could be administered Lakshmi Devi, Ashok and her daughter Kalyani, were kidnapped in the name of 'protection'. At that event she was given a proposal for conversion and a marriage proposition to a (Muslim) man. When this technique did not work she was abused in presence of her son and daughter. Afterwords a *Maulavi* Islamic preacher known to Lakshmi Devi provided shelter in a house adjacent to a Hindu *mandir* and asked her to convert to Islam. When she didn't agree to that proposal she was forced to spend nights with her would-be (Muslim) husband. Right after that Lakshmi Devi was forced to convert. She stayed back at a town near Iswardi as the number two wife of that man. Lakshmi was afraid that if she didn't agree this time around harm may befall on her little daughter Kalyani, the blissful. No mother can imagine this! Ashok told me that "In our heart we are still Hindu," and if I can find shelter for Kalyani in one of the Hindu-Buddhist dormitories. "No one would know that we are related to Kalyani."

"Are we still Hindu?" Mehboob asked us. "Of course if you believe I am a Hindu, why can't you think youreselves as Hindus?" I asked.

These days we find daily reports in newspapers of oppression of women: Muslim, Hindu, Christian, Buddhist, urbanites, tribal. Nevertheless, although minorities constitute only 13% of the population, however they constitute about 50% of the rape victims. Books on women and the newspapers of (the Bangladeshi cities) of Dhaka, Chittagong, Sylhet and Rajshahi provide the evidence. Because of the narrow mindedness of the Hindus those rape victims are being raped again by the Hindu community: the village, *para* neighborhood, family and the society consider these victims as 'guilty' and then they reject them. In this respect the liberalism (of multiple marriages) of the Muslim society has helped the (rape) victims. During the liberation war of 1971 thousands upon thousands of women and girls were oppressed and became pregnant by Pakistani (Army), anti-independence Bengali (Islamists) and by Urdu-speakers. Vast majority of them were Hindu. Responding to a call by *Bangabandhu*, meaning Friend of Bengal (affectionately addressed Sheikh Mujibur Rahman, the

Father of the Nation), thousands of men came forward to take these ladies back to our society. Of late there have been some changes in the Hindu (including Buddhist and Christian) society. In stead of making them castaways, these victims are being taken back to their families, villages and societies. Their names are also being printed in police and newspaper reports. Names and whereabouts of these hapless women can now be found in daily newspapers and in various editions or the book, *Nirjatan O Nipiraner Kichu Tathya* (Some facts and documents about torture and persecution {of minorities}) published from Dhaka.

Once I came to know of a landless peasant, Mrs. Mrinalini Dakua, of a traditionally Hindu oppressed caste. While conversing she told me that she was thinking of fleeing to India. When asked about herl destination she said, "I do not know." When I asked about the reason, she said, "My oldest daughter Anjali had just turned fourteen."

After the cremation of Niva, Kamalda planned to go to the city leaving Purnima in the village with her *Didima*, maternal grandmother. In our *desh* homeland and village news spreads through the thin air. Within hours of Purnima return to the village holding her grandpa Kamaldadu's hand that same *Maulavi* Islamic preacher appeared; this time with several young men. Their request, they want Purnima's "just for a few days." They would treat Purnima "like his own daughter." This time around it was a respectful request, not an order. Purnima tightly held her Kamal grandpa's hands and pleaded "Grandpa *Dadu*, please don't leave me behind. Ma will also protect us from the heavens."

Chapter 2

Doll's Wedding

(A)

'A girl is a jewel, *kanya-ratna*' — is a proverb in Bengal. It is believed that if the first born child of a family is a girl, then the household is blessed by the entry of both the Goddess of Wealth Lakhsmi, and the Goddess of Learning Saraswati. There is no better way of getting the blessings of Ma Lakhsmi and Ma Saraswati. But sadly enough, now-a-days a girl has become burden to many parents instead of blessing. For sometime now we have heard of the word, *Kanyadai-grastha*, 'burdened with a daughter.' With advancement of science the killing of female fetuses are progressing well. To prevent this barbaric act, laws have been passed (in India), but law? That's for another time. *Maya-devi*, Mrs. Maya, was never influenced by the narrow-mindedness of the modern Hindu mind. Even before her marriage she had a desire for girl, just like most of the American women. Life is not complete without a daughter.

Maya first saw her husband Daya on the night of her wedding. She got to chat with him on that night. Her marriage took place at a late *lagna* auspicious time.[1] On one hand there was joy and related tension, all-day fasting, socializing teasing and jokes of the groom's family, the smoke of the *home yajna* sacred fire — the vow and ritual that take place there, and on the other hand apprehension for spending the night with a complete stranger. Both mind and body were tired, concerned and nervous. After they had bolted the door of *Basar Ghar*, the decorated room the

---

1. The auspicious *lagna* time is set by astrologers which may last for a few minutes to a few hours, beginning in early evening to late night, before sun rise.

newlyweds spend the first night, none of them spoke for few moments. It was Daya who initiated conversation with questions whose answers he already knew. Though they were strangers to each other, they knew each others intimate details through their brothers, sisters, aunts, uncles and friends. There was nothing unknown to them. They knew quite well of each others favorite songs, poems, writers, novelists and even about teachers and subjects. Of the few unknown subjects they discovered is that both of them had love for a jewel: girl.

The marriage between Maya and Daya was arranged all of a sudden. Maya's family was quite educated, and for many generations. At the time of Bankim Chandra[2] Maya's grandfather's grandfather went to Presidency College. Maya's mother *Aparna-devi*, Mrs. Aparna, used to teach at the village school at their Baokati village of Barisal district in East Bengal, now Bangladesh. Years back she graduated from Calcutta University with a degree in economics. She became the headmistress of the Patit Paban & Iswari Kuiya Balika (girls) Bidyaloi (school). Now-a-days most folks know the school as P.P.I. School. Once there was a proposal from Muslims to change the Hindu oppressed caste name of the founders (to an Islamic) *Pir*[3] Piroj Islami School, at last it stuck as P.P.I. School. A while ago someone covered the name 'Patit Paban O Iswari Kuiya' in front of the school with paper. There were lots of people who said they were waiting for Aparna's death. *Aurobindo-babu*, Aurobindo, father of Aparna, after a transfer, taught for many years at the nearby Bakharganj College in southern coast of East Bengal, now Bangladesh. Mr. Aurobindo was a learned man,

---

2. Bankin Chandra Chattopadhyay was a litterateur, Indian nationalist and a pioneer of modern Indian writing. He was the first graduate of the first British-established Western-style college in India, Presidency, (1857).

3. *Pir* means Islamic saint.

writer and an author of many books. He raised their children with
prejudice-free open mind. He promised that he will send their
daughters for higher education. Amidst great difficulty he made
his eldest daughter Jaya a physician. Middle daughter Chaya
became an engineer from Dhaka Engineering University located
at the national capital. He wanted Maya to study at Calcutta
University, in now-foreign India, like her mother. It was really
difficult, as it was the rule of Pakistan then. Aunt Dipali *Pishi*, the
younger sister of Mr. Aurobindo, who lived in *Bagha Jatin*
Bengali Hindu Refugee Colony of Calcutta, wrote "please send
Maya here, we'll take care of her". But Aurobindo knew very
well that once he sends Maya to Calcutta, Pakistan Government
may not allow her to return home. He didn't want her to be sent
to *banabash* exile[4] in the forest called Calcutta. He had planned
for his daughter to become a scientist after obtaining an M.A.,
and then a doctorate degree. Storms blew over the family after
the Hazrat-Bal anti-Hindu killing of 1964, and after the Indo-
Pakistan war of 1965. There were tremendous loss to the family;
moreover, the children lost years from their education. More of
that another time. He somehow managed his life back to normal
till the 1970 Pakistan General Election. He almost forgot his misery
after hearing the '*Joi Bangala*' slogan.[5] Then came 26th of March
of 1971.[6] The family was targeted for killing by their Muslim
neighbors. At first they went from the town to a nearby village

---

4. As Lord Ram Chandra in the epic Ramayan went to *banabash*, living
   in forest, exile into Dandakaranya Forest.
5. In 1970 the first General Election of Pakistan was held when the
   nationalist Awami League Party received majority of seats in then
   united Pakistan. Their slogan was *Joi Bangla*, Victory to Bengal.
6. On that day Pakistan Army started military action against its majority
   Bengali population, and genocide against her Bengali Hindus.
   Bangladesh observes this as the Independence Day, when they
   declared independence.

seeking shelter. Then to Shibpur village. Thereafter to towns of Matlab, Chouddagram (in eastern Bangladesh), Belonia (of Tripura state of northeast India), then Reflugee Camp No.7 in Tripura state. There the family met Daya's family. At that time Daya was studying medicine at Mymensingh (in north-central Bangladesh), and Maya was about to appear at the college Intermediate Examination. Pakistani President Yahya Khan had openly declared killing of all the Hindus and ordered arrest of pro-secular, pro- independence Awami League Party followers. In this barbaric act of Pakistani Administration and Military Bengali Muslims joined in the garb of Muslim League, Al-Badr, and Al Shams[7] para-military death squads. Maya eventually came to Aunt Dipali *Pishi*'s home, but not to study but to wear *sankha* wedding bangles and wedding *sindur* vermilion mark on her scalp. Darling Maya was married at a lower age than her mother Aparna. Neither Aurobindo nor Maya had planned for it. The plan was broken but not the dream. Everybody said, "This must be God's *ashirbad* blessing. What a wonderful family, and a wonderful boy. Under pressure, human beings have to do many things." After marriage the couple Daya and Maya established themselves after completing their studies. Yet, Maya could never forget that she couldn't complete her studies from her parent's home.

(B)

Maya became pregnant soon after her marriage. Both husband and wife wished for a girl, their jewel *kanya-ratna*. They had elaborate discussions about the naming their daughter. Many names were suggested to them. Many in the family suggested '*Bharati*' in honor of unblemished support and affection of Bharat (India) during their independence struggle. Moreover, there was another reason for that name as Maya became pregnant at a refugee camp

---

7. Al Badr and Al Shams were the paramilitary killers of Hindus and Muslim Awami League leaders.

at Debigram in India. Some suggested she should be named
'*Debi*,' goddess, from Debigram, village of the goddess. Some
suggested 'Jaya' after 'Joi Bengla' slogan of the independence
struggle. Maya-debi, objected "What is that? How can you name
a niece after her aunt Mashi?" Mashi means mother's sister, i.e.
Maya's sister. In Bengali society people do not keep name of a
child after an older person. In the West it is just opposite. One's
name may be the same as of his father, grandfather, son, grandson
and great-grandson, for example, John Doe. The only difference
may be in John I, John II, John III and so forth. But the nicknames
have to be different. In case of women, however, the problem is
somewhat different. As women take their husband's last name,
they don't have to write I, II or III. But it is not uncommon to find
mother, daughter or aunt having the same name: Mary or Roslyn
or Laura. Back home such examples are rare. Many more names
were suggested to them, Mukti, Durga, Nandini, Durgesnandini,
Shyamolee, Joyeeta and so many others. Parents, Maya and Daya
both liked Bharati. But many said, "It is better that you don't
keep that name. (Anti-Hindu) communalists would say, 'You
people are Hindu. You love India, that's why you have kept that
name.' Daya couldn't imagine that in 1971 someone could say
this as his homeland gained independence after the sacrifice of
7,000 Indian lives! He used to say, "Communal thinking has been
finished forever from the life of the Bengali. The '*Joi Bangla*,'
Victory to Bengal, slogan had united both the Hindus and Muslims
forever. Auti-Hindu Pakistani, Islamic, Al-Badr and Al-Shams
groups are finished eternally. This '*Joi Bangla*' was able to instill
a sense of new hope in Daya in spite of the fact that he witnessed
first-hand killing and maiming of many Hindu families by Muslims,
their homes and properties confiscated.

Ending a long suspense, the home was brightened by the arrival
of Lord *Bishnu*, God of Preservation, instead of Ma Lakshmi.
The formal male name given to the baby was Debal, godly, instead

of Debi or Bharati, and the nickname was Bharot, the name of one of the brothers of epic Mahabharat. At the blessings of Ma Shasti (Goddess of Fertility) six more sons were born: Kajal, Sajal, Subal, Probal, Bimal and Dwipal. At last Goddess Lakshmi appeared at the home as a beautiful, lovely doll-like daughter, fulfilling the hope of the family. After calling the baby by many names, on the day of *Anna-prasan*, the rice eating ceremony, Grandma *Thakurma*[8] said, "That name 'Putul' or Doll, sounds real nice for the baby. It matches very well with my other grandkids." Many others used to call Putul by '*Satbhai Champa*,' the magnolia-like tropical *Champa* flower with seven brothers, by singing the famous song of Lata Mangeshker. Besides there were about 108[9] names like *Burri* (Toothless Old Lady), *Chhutki* (The Little Ones), *Takas-takas* (The Chatterer One), *Koler Meyey* (Baby Daughter on the Lap), Debi, Kali (Black Goddess), and more. As the father wrote Putul at the forms for the admission to school, that name finally stayed forever, while others slowly faded away. No doubt she really looked like a foreign doll when her curly hair was tied with a red ribbon on top of her round face, long wide eyes and her beautiful shining dark complexion. "The only difference was that the dolls in the market were too pale like Western *sahibs*, not like us," was a regular comment. The Baby Doll was so favorite of her seven immediate brothers, numerous aunts, uncles, other cousin brothers and sisters of that single-kitchen extended family that for years Putul rarely touched the ground leaving the arms of her loved ones.

Doctor Dayamoy had a good reputation in his profession. After working in this city and that city, this district and that district, he finally started his practice at Narayangonj city at his *Pishey*, father's

---

8. Father's mother.
9. In Hindu mythology all the gods and goddesses have 108 names, each describing some attributes and powers of them. *Burri*, *Chhutki*, etc. are very common affectionate nicknames for the girls.

sister's husband, Uncle's advice and encouragement. Having
Pishey Uncle's practice nearly was a big help, and after his
retirement all of his patients moved to Doctor Daya. Soon Daya's
fame as a physician had spread far and wide. In the beginning of
Daya's practice he had rented the large two storied house of the
Nandis, a Hindu, at the Jogi Satinath Das[10] Lane of Kolutala[11]
neighborhood. Kolutala was basically a Hindu area in the Muslim
nation. And Dr. Daya's medical office was at the nearby *Guptapara* (Gupta neighborhood). By cycle rickshaw this was a five
minute ride or less. Guptapara too was a Hindu neighborhood,
but all along Christians lived with Hindus. There are two churches
at Guptapara. One Catholic, the other was Protestant. And there
were Hindu mandir temples, big and small, at various nook and
cranny. Now Muslim mosques as well. Most Hindus and Muslims
didn't understand the differences of those churches, and used to
call both as Catholic churches. St. Mary's Girls School run by the
Catholic Church was very popular with the Hindus. Now, of
course, there are many Muslim girls who go to that school as lots
of Muslim families now live here. This change started to occur
after the terrible anti-Hindu Hajrat Bal killing of 1964. Then during
the Pakistan-India war of 1965 a large number of Hindu families
were forcibly evicted by confiscating their ancestral homes through
the use of Enemy Property Act by declaring patriotic Hindus as
'enemies of the state.' This continued till 1970. Then came the
Bangladesh Liberation War of 1971, and subsequent independence.
At the time of the Liberation War, Daya joined a medical team of
the Liberation Army, *Mukti-joddha*, in North Bengal. Kolutala
neighborhood was old and congested, in comparison houses at
Guptapara were quite big, like garden-homes, and also relatively
new, perhaps built during the thirties and forties. There was a touch
of *bonedi* aristocratic tradition in that area.

10. Jogi (*Yogi*) Satinath Das is a Hindu name.
11. Neighborhood of the *Kolus*, a traditionally oppressed-caste Hindu.

When Daya-*babu* and Maya-*debi* started living at Narayangonj all the seven sons were studying at various levels. Within a few years three of them lived elsewhere, married and well-settled. Debal was a physician at Dhaka, the national capital. Kajal was in Chittagong, the large port city, and Sajal was in the States. Subal was studying architecture in Dhaka, and was searching for jobs. Everybody used to praise his skill, in drawing and his concepts of design. Probal was studying business management in India, and people thought that he might settle somewhere over there, Bombay or Bangalore or Ahmedabad. Maya was able to find a teaching job immediately after her arrival. St. Mary's Girls School wanted her, but before that offer, hearing her arrival Trustee Abani Bhusan Bandopadhyay of the Bosepukur Ananda-Sundari Brahmo Mandir school of the adjacent neighborhood was at her home, "Ma,[12] you are like my daughter. I came running to you. I am addressing you as '*tumi*,'[13] 'you' for the younger person, please do not mind. My name is Abani Bhusan Bandopadhyay. It is our Creator Ma Durga's blessing to find a teacher like you. You always stood first, even after marriage, after you had children when you may have studied under great difficulty. Are these minor achievements? Mr. Rajib Karai, a close friend of mine, of the school at Bogura where you used to teach told me about you. Have you heard of Karai-babu, Mr. Karai?"

Maya pulled her sari *ghomta* hood a bit, then touched the feet of Abani Bhusan, "Uncle *Mesho-mashai*, who doesn't know of Advocate Karai of Jaipurhat in North Bengal? Who hasn't heard of *Karai-ukil* (attorney)? He was the one who has been protecting us like Mother Kali. He is like the proverbial shelter-giving banyan

---

12. Ma or Mother is an affectionate call for younger girls and ladies.
13. In Bengali, as in most Indian languages, there are three forms of you. '*Tumi*' is addressed to known younger or close individuals. For unknown persons it is the formal '*Aapni*.'

tree. Only God knows what would have happened to us had he not been there. Do you know how many times he was targeted for killing? Just before coming here, I heard of you from our Sir,[14] teacher." There were lots of other issues discussed. On the following day came Father Adhikari and Sister Pamela from St. Mary's Girls School.

(C)

Year rolled by. The number of people living in that big house has dwindled, and it was becoming difficult for Dayas to look after that large property. For a while Dayas were thinking of building their own home, instead of renting. Opportunity knocked. It was the house of Moni Mohan Datta, a Hindu, in Neetai Basak Road at Guptapara right next to his chamber (medical office). It was a *bagan-bari*, garden-house, but no one lived there. Moni Mohon had two sons, both of whom were living elsewhere. The old man and his wife lived there, but frequently they lived at Lakhsmi-bazar neighborhood in Dhaka, with their youngest son. Youngest son Ajit wanted to buy land with the sale of their Narayangonj home to build garment factory at Mohammadpur in Dhaka.

This was their first home after Barisal! Mr. Abdul Rahman, a Muslim, was the right neighbor who now lived at the home of Mrs. Swapna Mukherjee, a Hindu. In the next Ananta Aich's home now lived Munirujjaman Kamal Bachhu, a Muslim. Mrs. Kusum Nayek, a Hindu, lived next. All of them are Daya's patient. Next to Nayeks lived Narahari Ball, a Hindu. In the left narrow lane lived Paul Razario, a Christian; Haranath Mondol, a Hindu and right across lived Parasar Mitra and Kamana Chakraborty, both Hindu. They are also his patients. Moving close to known people Dayas felt this must also be like 'returning home,' back to

14. All male teachers are referred as Sir.

Barisal in coastal Bangladesh. There is a lot of mental agony in selling one's ancestral property. Moni Mohan Duttas shed a lot of tears thinking about selling thier ancestral home, but nobody in the area knew about that. They were afraid if outsiders knew that a Hindu wa; contemplating selling their home, then Muslims would have forcibly taken over. "Whatever you might think, this is Hindu property," many Muslims used to say. "Why should we buy it with our money? We'll get it anyway."

Once Duttas learned that Dayas were in the market for a home, *Moni-babu*, Mr. Moni, and his wife Satya-*debi*, Mrs. Satya, almost the age of Daya's parents, arrived at their Satinath Das Lane home of Kolutala, unannounced. They came real early, almost before the birds started chirping, lest others find out. Giving a gift of a pitcher full of *rasagolla*, a syrup filled cheese-ball sweet, they begged, "Ma, You are a true incarnation of Goddess Durga. We understand that you have a Mother Saraswati, Goddess of Learning, in your home in your daughter Putul, besides you have Lord Kartick and Lord Ganesh, sons of Goddess Durga, with you as well. We've heard that Putul is a brilliant student, and always gets a top rank. Your family is the pride of our family as well!"

"Yes, *Mesho* Uncle, Putul is like the precious eye-ball[15] of all of her elder brothers. And her father too wants that she goes for higher studies. Her elder brothers want her to go to America for higher education. Please bless her so that she may not be married early like me." Maya and Daya welcomed the strangers by touching their feet.

Finally they raised the issue. "You all please come to our house. There will be no better fate for us over this. Pay us as you like;

---

15. *Chokher moni*, the eye-ball, is an expression for extremely beloved persons.

and if you cannot pay, still come."

"How can we live, if we cannot pay *Mesho* Uncle? Moreover, we have decided not to buy any house if the owner intends to flee to India after selling it to us. Even if it is given free to us. A number of Hindu families at Kolutala want to sell us their home."

"No, no, my child, we will be staying here. Our Dhaka house is also a family property of many generations. Now-a-days we do not have extended family system. How long can we hold on to our properties? Moreover, we have only two sons. Sushanto lives in Dhaka and Prosanto lives overseas."

Dr. Daya's popularity had been increasing in Narayangonj by the day. In his house now lived three teenagers: Bimal, Dwipal and Putul. Bimal is going to a private university and Dwipal and Putul are in high school.

(D)

Thakur, Hindu priest, suggested that the *Rathayatra,* Chariot Festival, day is auspicious for *Griha-prabesh,* house entering, sort of house-warming ceremony; accordingly arrangements were made. They decided to have a big celebration. Not only all the sons' families were coming but also friends and relations were coming from Barisal, Khulna, Bogura, Sylhet in Bangladesh, and even from bordering Agartala (Tripura state), Dhubri (Assam) and Calcutta (West Bengal) in India. If one leaves aside refugee homes at *jabar-dakhal* forcibly occupied private land in Agartala, Dhubri and Calcutta, this was the first time that someone was entering their own home since grandfather entered his own. Everyone said "It is no small matter."

The Bose family living a cross brought Nayan *Dhaki,* Nayan the *(Dhak)* drum player, from their ancestral village the night before. "Nayan-*babu*, Mr. Nayan, was a very deft *Dhak* player." Along came his brother Subhas and the youngest son Kanti.

For the last couple of days the house was quite festive. There was the atmosphere of happiness all around, it was almost like the mood of a marriage ceremony. When the drums were played in the morning during the *home yajna* ritual with the Eternal Fire, it almost felt like Durga Puja festivities in the fall month of *Aswin*, instead of the current monsoon month of *Aashar*.The main feast was to be at mid-day. Old as well as new acquaintances all had kept their dates, although it drizzled all day. No one was missing from the invitation list. Some of the women worked in the kitchen the entire day, as if they were friends for a long time. Lots of help is needed for such occasions, as it is said one needs a thousand pair of hands, for cooking, peeling and cutting of vegetables, arragement for puja service, cutting fruits, plucking flowers, knitting garlands, arranging special *noibidya* offering at puja service, cooking *bhog* sacred food to be offered to God, blowing of conches, breakfast and continually making tea, and millions of other chores. Then one has to think who's going to sleep where, transporting them, taking back-and-forth the priest, and welcoming guests.

The evening *Arati*, the greeting of deity by waving lamp and other objects, was being performed in the living room. It was packed with people, not even an empty space for a step. Many women also sat in the big bedroom, while men sat under the tent set up in the front garden. People sitting included from near and far, relatives and non-relatives, Hindus, Muslims, Christians, Buddhists, poor and not-so-poor. Everyone was enjoying the sounds of *Kansar Ghanta* — the round iron disc hit with a striker, the smell of burning of festive *dhup-dhuna* incense and resins. Daya and Maya were running around in circle. In the midst of this the youngest son Taimur of Abdul Rahman, the Muslim neighbor living in Swapna Mukherjee's home, softly pulled Maya's *anchal* sari-end. Maya could not feel it at first, but he must have pulled

3

several times. "Babu, do you like to say something to me or to your *Chacha*[16] Uncle?"

From minor cold to fever, Mr. Abdul *Sahib* and his wife Afroza Khanam Rozie used to send scores of folks to the Doctor for free medicine and treatment, from the days when Dayas were living in the other neighborhood. After they bought the house, and for these months they have been living at two places, it was difficult to remember as to now many times Taimur came to them. At first they used to send Sarfarat, a few years senior to Putul. Finally Maya told Afroza, "*Bhabi,* sister-in-law, why do you have to send Sarafat? If you send your servent Muhammad, it'll do. Moreover, the Chamber of Putul's dad is next to your house." When needed the doctor used to supply them free medicine, syrup and prescription. Abduls had lots of money, but all of that made through 'No. 2 means.' The house of Swapna Mukherjee that they are living now was forcibly occupied by evicting the Hindu owners. Abdul himself used to proudly proclaim, "Although the house belonged to a *Malu,*" a derogatory word derived from the Arabic *Malaun* used against the lowly, sub-human, infidel Hindus, "I still paid 10,000 takas," a tiny fraction of the actual price, "for this house." He used to tell everybody that "at that time the house was worth at least 1,400,000 to 1,500,000 takas." But he never used to say that to Hindus or Christians. This they told so times to the Muslim neighbor, Manirujjaman Kamal Bachchu and his wife Khaleda Bokul.

Maya-*debi* said again, "What do you want *Babu?* Why don't you go upstairs, there are many friends?"

"Aunt *Khalamma, Abba,* father, asks you to stop the *ghanta* bell, and conch blowing. If we hear that (Hindu celebration) it brings *guna,* inauspiciousness, sin."

"What did you say, *Babu*? I couldn't follow."

---

16. A Muslim term for uncle, father's brother.

"*Abba* said to stop the *ghanta* bell, and conch blowing. If we hear that it brings *guna,* inauspiciousness, sin."

"Okay. Why don't you go now? I'll see."

After Taimur left, Maya took Daya to the small room in the second floor, bolted it, then whispered him the words. That evening no one else knew of this.

(E)

Quite a few years have passed in this new house, yet it fills like "We've arrived just the other day." Time has passed with pleasure and pain, especially when Rahmans are your next door neighbor. Among the youngsters only two are left at home, Dwipal and Putul. Dwipal is now going to college and Putul is appearing in School Final Exam. Daya's tension was rising as his dear Doll was growing up, as were of her elder brothers. One of them came one day and said "I know of a suitable match." The next week he'd say, "you can't marry untill you are done with your studies. There won't have any dearth of suitable match." Then the other brothers would say, "She's our only sister, the youngest one, she doesn't need to worry about this." From abroad Sajal and Probal were sending prospectus and admission forms from different colleges in America and India. With the arrival of each of those forms, Daya's blood pressure would rise. On one hand he wants Doll to continue her studies but on the other he can't think of loosing Putul from home. Same has been true for Putul's *Borda,* eldest brother, *Mejda,* the middle brother and Dhanoda,[17] the third eldest brother. Whenever Daya raises the issue of Putul's marriage, Maya responds angrily and reminds Daya of their own marriage. "Don't you remember? You said that you'll have Putul go for higher studies before she marries. It is a sin for us to think

---

17. It is customary for younger persons to call older persons by relationship, not by their first name..

of her marriage when she's only sixteen or eighteen." Daya used to become silent, even more reflexive. One side of his heart struggled with the other side.

On the last evening of Putul's exam her brother's family started arriving at their home. The Doll belongs to everyone, a Doll to play with, everyone wants. Nobody wants to give it up, but it is dawning on them that for higher studies their Doll was about to leave home. Nobody cared to know what Putul wished. For some reason, Daya was convinced that at the instigation of her mother and two elder brothers Putul is excited to leave home. In the evening he returned from his chamber a bit early and went straight to Putul's room and started conversation: about exam, questions, results, friends, brothers, holiday plans, and more.

Putul didn't like idea of dad returning home early. She found him to be restless. "Baba, Dad, are you all right? When Borda arrives, I'll ask him to take a look at you." Putul knew very well that her father was sad because of her.

"I am all right, though there's too much work, and this incessant rain. Let me take two aspirins and rest a while. Everything will be fine." He went to his bedroom. Taking a bowl of *murri* puffed rice and a cup of tea from *Gopaler Ma,* Gopal's Mother, the family maid, although Putul herself took it to her father. At night it took a lot of hollering to wake him up from the bed. He took bits of food and aspirin again and went to bed. Kajal and Subal came at night, thus the gossiping went till late. Nobody knew how late. But they all had to wake up very early because of mother's scream, she was unable to wake father up.

(F)

After completing the *sraddha* memorial ceremony and *matsya-mukh,*taking of the first non-vegetarian food, fish, after the memorial on the 13th day of the mourning, all had to return to work. It was decided that Probal would go to holy Gaya in India to offer *pinda* sacramental food to the departed and to other ancestors, and Kajal would go to Sitakunda in Bangladesh, the holy abode of Mother Kali, which was a favorite place of Daya. On every opportunity, he used to visit that place.

Once Sajal was taken to catch the morning bus, the entire house seemed eerily quite, pin-drop silent, desolate, lifeless and helpless. There is only one less person. There were Maya, Dwipal, Putul and Gopal's Mother. Basanti's Mother came in the mornings and afternoons for part-time domestic help. Still it was the feeling of loneliness, helplessness. Dwipal and Putul were both teenagers, and Maya was the only adult. In a few days Kajal came to take Putul away for holidaying at their home.

It was Friday, the weekly holiday, and Dwipal went out with his friends. Gopaler Ma was hanging cloths on the back. At the sound of opening of the outside gate Maya looked up and saw her neighbor Mr. Abdul Rahman coming towards the house. He was possibly returning after the mid-day *Jumma* Friday Muslim *Namaz* prayer. He was wearing blue checked *lungi* bottom covering, a long calf-length *punjabi* shirt embroidered at the neck and a white prayer cap on his head. Maya-*devi* barely had time to pull her sari *ghomta* hood over her head before Rahman arrived. He gave her a Muslim *salam*, and said, "*Adaab*," an Arabic Islamic greeting, "I thought you must be feeling lonely, so I have come to see you. It is a blessing of Allah that I have such good neighbor like you. This is Allah's doing. We are very happy with you."

"Won't you be seated? Can I offer you a cup of tea?" Immediately after saying Maya hollered, "Gopaler Ma."

"No, no, there is no need for that. I left home after breakfast;

I'll eat after returning home. Let me come back to what I wanted to tell you. We all watched Putul to grow up as a lady before our eyes. *Dada,* my older brother, your husband, told me that she might go elsewhere for higher studies. *Daktar Sahib,* the doctor, I heard thought of her marriage as well."

Before he could finish Maya interrupted Rahman, "No, no, Is this an age for marriage? I was married young. Please bless her so that she might become like her father. Her father really liked Apratim, the youngest son of his friend Tridib Nanda of Jessore. He had a top rank in the Board's exam. *Tridib-babu,* Mr. Tridib, also likes Putul. Then, all of a sudden *Tridib-babu's* wife Ratnadi, older sister Ratna, passed away. If Putul becomes a wife in that family her father's soul would find peace, *shanti.* So, please bless her."

"Of course. But, what's the use in marrying into a mother-dead *Nomo,* low caste untouchable, family?"

Maya knew that 'Nomo' is slur for Hindus which these days one hears in the bazaars market places, schools and colleges, around the courts, everywhere and all the time. She thought, 'What is he saying? Rahman must have mistaken Nomo for Nanda.' Moreover, she had never ever heard the word 'untouchable' from any Hindu.

Rahman continued, "After the death of *Daktar Sahib,* I have prayed daily for such blessing. We are looking for a match for our son Sarafat. If married at a tender age the bride could be molded as our own (member of the family). He is interested in business. One could say that he practically runs my business. He has no interest in studies, and that's why he hasn't attended school for the past few years. But he is tutored at home by teacher Khalilur Sir." Nothing was entering Maya's head. Rahman continued saying, "We have connection with Hindus for a long time. My Nana, maternal grandma, was Hindu, from high caste. We also hail from high caste. We've Pathan blood in us. My Nana never allowed beef to enter our house.

"Whatever Taimur told you earlier about me with regards to puja service, *ghanta* bells, conch blowing those were little boy's mischievousness. When I came to know of that from the Doctor, I chastised him a lot. I do not know from whom has he learnt all those. Don't mind children's pranks."

Mrs. maya was feeling dizzy, she thought she might faint. "Rahmán *Sahib,* please wait, my oven is going to catch fire....."

"No, you go, I've to leave as well. But think of the proposal. This is Allah's wish. Putul is like my own daughter, at our home Sarafat's Ma will treat her like a queen. We're progressive people, we do not discriminate between Hindus and Muslims. Once you perform *Tablig*, Islamic conversion, then all the troubles are over. You won't need to change her name. There is the name Putul in our own family."

In the evening Rahman's wife Afroza arrived with a pitcher full of sweets. "Oh, Gopaler Ma, Did I hear that Maya-*bhabi,* sister-in-law, isn't feeling well? That's why I am here."

Gopaler Ma couldn't think what to say. After a bit of hesitation she said, "*Khalamma,* maternal aunt, Ma can't come now. She is at her *puja* meditation; it'll take time."

(G)

After Abdur Rahman left Maya took to the bed. She could not decide whom to tell all these. 'Should I call Debal at Dhaka? Or, Kajal at Chittagong? No, there's Putul with them. But Dwipal should be told, but no one knows when he is going to return. He has gone out with his friend.' She was thinking about these, and many other things.

Gopaler Ma was guarding Maya-*debi*. She was lying down

bloking Maya's bedroom door, with Maya's meal, by the side of her bed. Every five minute she was reminding Maya to eat. She is a mother herself, so it was not difficult for her to realize that there's something wrong somewhere. "What has happened Ma, are you feeling sick? Are you feeling sad because of Putul? Did Rahman *Sahib* give you any bad news? Should I call *Borrda,* the eldest brother? If you don't have any problem, please tell me. No one will know except the Lord, *Thakur.*" Gopaler Ma too did not eat anything but a few handful of *murri* puffed rice. She didn't ask Basantir Ma to come to that side. She left after cleaning a few utensils, and sweeping only the downstairs.

After Basantir Ma left Maya entered *Thakur Ghar,* the shrine room and lighted the evening lamp, blew the conch. She handed over the incense stand to Gopaler Ma and asked "please come back to me after the daily *Sandhya* ritual," showing the burning incense around the house. "You're a member of my own family, I have something to share."

Following *Sandhya* ritual, Maya told everything to Gopaler Ma. "No, Mother I can't allow this to happen. Those are Satans. He hasn't completed even sixth grade. Do you know how many times has he failed promotion? Mr. Kamaluddin Sinha, who's sort of a *Dulabhai* brother-in-law, and lives at Bakultala neighborhood, tells that they are now engaged in thuggery, bootlegging, and confiscation of Hindu properties. Local boys call them by all sort of ugly names. What business? We're here for so long, have you seen anything? If asked of businesses, they only name (cities of) Dhaka, Sylhet or Khulna. Of late they are into smuggling to India. *Dulabhai* says they are after girls. It is said that if they convert Hindus to Islam, then they receive *chhowab,* Allah's blessing. No Muslim will give them their daughter. Why are they after my daughter? Ask them, are they willing to marry their daughters in our families?" As Gopaler Ma was saying, her body was shivering with rage. In the midst of this Afroze Begum or Mrs. Rahman or Rozie *Sahiba* shouted her arrival.

(H)

Without telling anyone the following Tuesday evening Rahman and his son Sarafat appeared at Kajal's apartment at Chittagong. "We were around, so we thought we'd drop by. Ma Putul is here, isn't she?"

Kajal's wife Shyamolee opened the door. Before she answered Kajal arrived. "Why are you visiting our place, Rahaman *Sahib*? Where did you get our address? Are you here for any special reason?"

"No. We thought we'd see our Doll. I've brought Sarafat. Didn't your mother tell you anything?"

"Rahman Sahib, for heaven's sake don't ask us about Putul. She is our youngest sister, very dear to us. She is not a doll of your imagination, but a woman of flesh and blood. Her wish is above everything else. We are a bit busy now." But he added, "Do you want to have a seat? Would you like to come another day?" To be polite Kajal said these, as he was of his father's age, that's why.

Mr. Rahman said tauntingly, "Are you playing with a doll now? Very good. But would you be able to protect her? See that the doll is not broken, I have a propensity to break things."

A call came Thursday morning. The elder brother of a local Member of Parliament was making the call. "*Aapa*, Sister, do you recognize me? I am M.P. Akkach Ali's *Barrobhai* elder brother Ikram Khan Hira. I have met you many times. I've just learnt that your son Kajal has insulted Rahaman *Sahib*. He went to Kajal's home with a marriage proposal for his son Sarafat. He didn't even offer him a seat. They are very influential people. They are members of the Party. Try to keep good relations with them. Make sure that it doesn't turn into the situation like Aparajita, daughter of Professor Amit Basu, a Hindu. That girl is now wife of Khairul, a Muslim. Their house is occupied by Anam, a Muslim, and I understand they are now live in a slum in India. I wish you well, that's why I am saying this."

A few days later Putul came to visit her mother for a night before heading to *Borda* Debal at Dhaka. It was decided that she would continue her studies from there.

It was Thursday evening. May be a few weeks had passed by. Maya was doing Lakshmi puja service to the Goddess of Wealth. Downstairs Dwipal was watching TV with his friends Sayan, Afjal, Rana, Tapan, Jahangir and Montu, both Muslim and Hindu. Two women from the neighborhood Khaleda Bokul 'Aunty,' a Muslim, wife of Manirujjaman, and Kusum Nayek 'Aunty,' a Hindu, came in a hurry. "Is *Bhabi,* sister-in-law in?"

"Yes. She's doing *puja* prayer. Please go upstairs. Gopaler Ma , aunt Kamana *Pishi,* are also there. And perhaps aunt Mondal *Kakima.*" Dwipal showed them the way.

Kusum Nayek raised the issue right away. "Didi, (sister,) the news is bad. The Rahmans with their acomplices may go to Dhaka tomorrow in search of Putul after performing the *Magrib namaz.* They will take the *Imam,* Islamic preacher of the B.B. Road mosque of Banani area. At any cost do not allow Putul to stay with Debal tomorrow. If you can, bring her here, we're here. They won't dare do this here. It'll be better if you could soon complete the marriage with Apratim of Jessore.

Through Bokul's window they can hear everything from Rahman's home. After taking a deep breath Kusum and Bokul whispered a few more things.

Rahamans went to Dhaka as planned. Except for Mr. Subodh Chakraborty, a Hindu, the domestic help, no one else was there. They were at Jessore in Arindam's house. Through this jolt the marriage was settled at uncle Tridib *Mesho*'s house. There was an auspicious date within seven days. This time too it was held at a Bangladeshi Hindu refugee slum in Calcutta, India. Arindam flew straight to the Calcutta airport, just for just 48 hours. He couldn't come home to Jessore. As per Doll's wish, it was decided that she would stay home until she's done with her studies. She'd go to her husband after *Dwiragaman,* the first post-marriage return visit as married couple to the bride's parent's house. Just recently the *Dwiragaman* ceremony was held with big pomp and gaiety at their own home at Netai Basak Road of Gupta-*para* in Narayangonj City.

Chapter 3
Language Martyr's Day

According to a proverb, 'If there is a will, there is a way.' But it is also true that there are situations beyond one's will. One such wish for me was to attend Dhaka's 21st February Language Martyr's[1] day celebrations, especially after Bangladesh became independent (in 1971). But the type of job I do it is impossible to get leave in February, as I can't take holiday in the month of Aswin (in autumn) for Durga Puja. That's why I can't attend Durga Puja and Ekushey (Twenty-first) back home. In 1997, I unexpectedly got an opportunity to fulfill my unfilled dream during my sabbatical leave. But I wasn't able to get to Dhaka before 21st. At last I got an afternoon Calcutta-Dhaka ticket. I took that ticket; still it was like getting to New York for Macy's Thanksgiving Parade next day. I would miss the morning *Prabhat Ferry* procession, the *Pushpanjali* flower offerings and the morning *Mela* fair.

At last after touring six countries I reached the Singapore Airport to catch a flight for Calcutta. There I learned that the flight goes via Dhaka. But as my ticket was for Calcutta the airline authority would not allow me to get off at Dhaka. This I cannot do according to airline regulation. I pleaded with them, then some argument. A few minutes before boarding they offered me a boarding pass for Dhaka and said, "As you are carrying only a handbag, we are making this exception. Moreover, please sign

---

1. 21st February or Ekushey (twenty-first) is possibly the most important and sacred day in Bangladeshi calendar. On that day in 1952 Pakistan administration killed a number of Bengalis who were demanding that Bengali be declared a national language of Pakistan, then spoken by 55% of Pakistanis. Ultimately this movement resulted in the independence for the Bengalis.

here telling us that you won't seek refund for your Dhaka-Calcutta sector," and produced a paper for me to sign. In a hurry I could not contact anybody at Dhaka.

At the customs in Dhaka I met my friend Jahirul Islam, who had just arrived from London in another flight. And to receive Jahirul, Tajuddinda, brother Tajuddin, had come to the airport, with whom I was supposed to be staying in a few days. (Older brother) Tajda pinched me to see if I was real or a ghost.

In Dhaka the celebration starts from midnight of 8th of (the Bengali month) of Falgun, when the clock strikes twelve and the 21st (of February) begins. Although according to Bengali tradition the day begins at sunup, but that is a matter of tradition. I wished first to visit the martyr's monument *Shahid Bedi* in the middle of the night, then later in the morning. But Tajda, Lata-*baudi*, Lata (Tajuddin's wife), and others asked me not to try in the middle of the night as the *Shahid Bedi* monument area would be cordoned off for the dignitaries. Both Tajda and Lata-*boudi* said, "If you still insist, we could ask *Borda*, if he would be able to get a pass." Taj's *Borda*, his eldest brother, whom we call Ganida after his first name Gani, was a minister a few years back. Finally it was decided that I'll get up real early with Tajda, and after morning bath and his *Namaz* prayer, we would join a morning *Prabhat Ferry* procession at our neighborhood. The plan was executed as intended. At dawn Jamil, a domestic boy, woke me up, "Sir, here's hot water." Tajda said, "You finish your bath quickly. Then before we all are done with our baths, you complete the puja offering for the martyrs as Aunt Mashima, your mother, wished, at the Hindu *mandir* (temple) to take some blessed flowers to the *bedi* offering platform. Before I left Lata-*boudi* summoned me. I asked, "Finished your bath? Would you like to join?"

"No, not yet, but let me tell you the location of our local temple."

After reaching I found out that the *mandir* hadn't opened that early. Thereafter I went to the nearby Dhakeswari Mandir, the temple of Goddesss of Dhaka. There some folks had already assembled to join the morning *Prabhat Ferry* procession. But, what's this? I was totally unprepared for it! Why the 500-year old mandir is in ruins? I had assumed that the temple was repaired after the 1990 nationwide mass destruction of Hindu temples. Alas! I could not believe my own eyes. This was 1992, one and one-and-a-half year later. Afterwards (Muslim) Yusuf, Tajda, *Lata-boudi*, (Hindu) Niranjanda all of them said, "Had we known you'll be heading to Dhakeswari, we would have suggested not to go. But where else would we have asked you to go?" Yusuf added, "Our neighborhood Hindu *mandir* is in the same situation. We do not go to Hindu temples, so we don't know of their situation. The other day I escorted one of my friends, that's how I came to know of this. Looking at this we come to tears, and I can barely figure out the mental anguish of Hindus and Buddhists." On that trip, I was an eyewitness to destruction of Jaikali Mandir of Dhaka and of many other temples. And a few days later in 1993, I myself witnessed thousands of Hindu temples, homes, dormitories, cremation areas, businesses and shops destroyed. On that pogrom Dhakeswari Mandir was spared, but they torched *Puja Mandap* worship area and the *Natmandir*, the performance structure, were in the same condition. The (ancient) deity of Ma Dhakeswari hadn't returned, which didn't perish during the openly anti-Hindu era of Pakistan, but was lost during the Bengali rule. 1990-destroyed Shiva Temples located in the complex have now been repaired nicely. Dhaka Mahanagar (metropolitan) Puja Committee has been trying very hard to save this ancient *mandir*.

I returned home with a heavy heart. Within a short walk from home we're able to join with a morning *Prabhat Ferry* procession. Everybody's marching forward. Most women wore red-bordered white sari and some *salwar-kamij* loose-fitting pants and long shirt. Men had white *pajama* pants and *punjabi* shirts, but mostly wore trousers and shirts. I wanted to put on *dhuti* garment and *punjabi*, but some folks asked, "Why do you need that?.............But nothing will happen during *Prabhat Ferry* and at *Boi Mela* book fair". I came to Dhaka with a backpack after touring six countries; although I had a collar-less, loose-fitting, half-sleeve *fotua* shirt in my backpack, but I had no *dhuti*. I couldn't buy one the day before as the shops were closed due to a festival. Anyway, I left with Tajda with my jeans and a red *fotua*. Our *Prabhat Ferry* procession passed a cemetery. As we were getting closer to the monument the crowd was swelling. Some were signing songs, just like the *Poush Mela* (fair in the month of Poush i.e., December) of Santiniketan[2] (West Bengal, India). There were beautiful *Alpana* designs painted on the road surface. There were many banners, festoons and flags. People were paying respects for Jabbar, Salam, Barkat and many others who became martyrs. So many topics were being discussed. Though it was like on ocean of humanity, I never had the fortune of seeing such a disciplined crowd. Goddess of luck must have been happy with me.

The martyr's *Shahid Bedi* alter was covered with *Alpana* paintings. Volunteers were redecorating the *Alpana* with the flower bouquet that the guests were offering. On the background loud-speakers were making announcements and playing songs, and in the middle of people were offering their (Muslim) *salam* or (non-Muslim) *pranam* respect. At the *Shahid Bedi* alter Tajda and I sought permission from an official to take picture. The man surveyed us from head to toe, then asked some questions. After

---

2. Visva Bharati University, founded by poet Rabindranath Tagore, is located at Santiniketan (abode of peace). To save Indian culture from extinction Tagore institutionalized that tradition with an annual fair at Santiniketan.

a sort conference with other important persons he allowed us to stay at the alter for a little while. Tajda, his little daughter Ranu, and I took pictures at our hearts content; with our flower bouquets, marigolds, and with other flowers.

A few steps ahead was the *Boi Mela* book fairground at the Bangla Academy. Here I met with some old friends. Nurulda was on the dais. A few days ago Nurulda presented two of his books: one was on the life of artist Bulbul Chowdhury and the other on Nazrul.[3] We exchanged greetings through our eyes. Tajda introduced me with some intellectuals, including some writers and journalists. From there I joined (Hindu) Ramakrishna Mission's program at the invitation of Swamiji (head monk). After a brief stop, I went to the Islamic Book Fair at the city's grand Baitul Mukarram Mosque at the request of Kaium and Robin; after that, the Buddha *Mandir* temple at the invitation of Bhantey, the venerable monk. I touched a few more invitations, with my transport's engine running. On the same day I have to go to Comilla to attend Ramakrishna Orphanage's program at the invitation of its residents. To help them we've established a Probini Foundation, and through that we've been able to raise a few pennies, and already been able to take full responsibility of a few children. After staying at Comilla, 60 miles east, I have to go to Habigonj and Sylhet (in the northeast) next day. People say when the blood is hot one can do a lot. In other places people say that it is the effect of adrenalin. True. Otherwise how didn't I feel tired although I was rushing like a speeding bullet? Truly it was a win-win situation. Everything was 'win,' and there was no thought of loss, that's why.

At the request of my elders a few days earlier, I had thought of

---

3. Bengali poet Kazi Nazrul Islam of India, a rare individual, is a national poet of both India and Bangladesh.

offering flowers at the Kali temple at Ramna in Dhaka City. I went there a few days after my Comilla and Sylhet visit. Whoever I asked about the Ramna temple, everyone responded, "The temple is no longer there." Ramna Park is now renamed as Surawardy Park. "There's no need to go." "You won't like it," was the response from everybody, from Tajda to Swamiji, from *Jamaibabu*, brother-in-law, to the rickshaw driver, from Hindu Robin and Muslim Yusuf to Buddhist monk Bodhipal and sister Anjanadi. Some said "You won't even be able to locate the spot." It is true on earlier occasions I could not locate the place. This time I took Robin and his friend Muhammad, the gardener of that park, with me, without whom it would have been really impossible for me to locate the site. Had I not taken those pictures, I would have thought myself a liar. Not a single brick is there of that 1,000-year old Hindu temple. It was one of the most important ancient Hindu sites of greater Bengal. Even the old bathing *ghat* steps (to the temple pond), the old coconut trees, even the ashram of Ma Annadamoyee were destroyed.[4] Mohammad was giving me the oral history. Spotting a place on a grass Mohammad said, "Babu, Sir, here was the temple." Pointing his finger to another place he said, "Here was my father's *Akhra*,"a meeting place in Hindu temples for religious chanting and discourse. "Even now my father often visits this temple site." Wiping their eyes, both of them requested me, "Sir, please offer some flowers here. But first take off your shoes." Both Robin and Mohammad too offered flowers on bald space of the grass lawn that has been created in the temple site.

---

4. A late 1990 citizen inquiry commission revealed that over 100 Hindu devotees, monks and priests, visitors, men, women and children were burned alive when Pakistan Army and her Islamist supporters corralled the individuals and set them on fire. See, www.hrcbm.org for the report.

My father said "that 'until the temple is re-built here his soul will not get peace even after his death. And the nation too won't find peace.' There was talk of re-building the temple. Once a (military) Major brought along someone folks carrying lumber to build the temple. My father joined with them. I've heard that because of this crime the man was imprisoned for three years. Why can't you build a small temple as before? This belongs to our country. I am a Muslim, I want that too. I know some people are crying against this, but if the government wants, we can build it in a day or two.................."

On that Twenty-first, the Bengali language day, I was heading to Comilla on a 'non-stop' bus, enjoying the beautiful scenery. Bengali modern songs were being played. I was really enjoying it. The guy seated next to me did not hesitate to divulge his private information because, "we were his own people." I shared my lunch from my bag. He was all the more delighted. The tape stopped a while later. A man shouted "Brother, play *Bhatiali*[5] now." Someone inquired, "Do you have the tape of Sandhya?" Many such requests started coming. I said to myself, '*Anurodher Ashar*, the old radio program of listeners' request, is still continuing.' But surprising everybody bus started Hindi songs. Again many requests started pouring in for Bengali songs. I too joined with the crowd, "Brother, please play Bengali songs." The lady seating by the side let it be known that she is carrying tapes. From the other side came objection. "No, let's continue with Hindi." Even after that, came requests for Bengali song. To that some official came up with a slur, and after that the listeners' request stopped. Rest of the journey I kept remembering the martyrs for Bengali language and silently sang (the famous song of D. L. Roy):

---

5. A type of Bengali folk song associated with boatmen singing while rowing boat.

"Our pride, Oh our hope,

Oh my Bengali language..."

Returning to Calcutta I once told a (Bengali) intellectual that I "went to Dhaka to participate in the celebration of the Twenty-first." He asked me in English, "What is 21st ?" Why only in Dhaka, he could not believe that many people in Silchar city of Assam state of India have died for Bengali language. In January of 1993, a few days before the death anniversary of the famous Bengali writer Sarat Chandra Chattopadhyay, near his own home (called Sarat Smriti [memorial] Mandir [temple]) in the Bengali aristocratic Ballygunj neighborhood of Calcutta I asked for its location. The man replied me in English, "What Sarat Chandra?"

I said "Sarat Chandra Chattopadhyay, the famous litterateur." I got a response in English "I don't know any Mister Chattopadhyay."

I was a bit late reaching Comilla. In that evening as soon as I entered the orphanage, a bunch of kids came running to take me to the stage. To take my backpack there must have a dozen of stretched hands. This must be what is called 'Royal Welcome!' And it must be a huge luck to become a *Kaka* Uncle to so many boys. In my honor Shankar-babu, invited all the ashram residents, "Once again, start the prayer for him." Seventy-five kids joined in the tune of the harmonium;

This is my home, this is my *desh*,

This is my Bengal, Bangladesh.

I too joined the chorus.

Chapter 4
Meeting Raja and Reza Once Again

I know both Raja and Reza[1] quite well in that Muslim-majority land. They address me as *Kaku* or uncle, and they themselves are great friends of each other— almost one soul, one might say. Whenever I meet them it reminds me of another Bengali pair on the other side of the border: Somir Acharya, a Hindu with Bengali name, and Saamir Awolaad, a Muslim with Arabic name. Raja and Reza, Hindu and Muslim respectively, are of the same age and were born in the same village from two lower-middleclass families. Both were brilliant students, and alternatively occupied the top positions in the class. But howsoever connected they may be in their souls, the society have always wanted to pull apart their souls, without their knowldge and permission. I met them at my *desh* home in December 1992 and in January 1993 when effects of the anti-Hindu and anti-minority pogrom had not subsided altogether, large scale attacks on minorities may have gone down a bit but minor attacks were still continuing. At first I met their families in the city, and this story is about that. Although I found both of them quite disturbed, however, when I talked to their families it seemed to me that the families had come from two different planets or distinctly different countries. Why is this happening is my question to the journalists, intellectuals, bureaucrats, politicians, rulers and oppressors. Are we resorting to lies and bluff? Is the result of this good or bad?

At a home party where I was invited to all the discussants in unison suggested, "Nothing happened at home." And " if any *danga* (Muslim-Hindu) rioting took place, it must have happened

---

1 Raja means king in Bengali and in other Indian languages. Reza is a princely title in Persian.

in (faraway) Uttar Pradesh, Maharashtra and West Bengal states of India." Only exception was Muslim Reza and her little sister Basanti. Occasionally they protested and finally outraged Basanti let be known that an organization to which she belongs will soon publish a book about the pogrom with pictorial documentation. They received no support from their elders. A few of the guests at that party were very influential persons of the nation. They also let be know, "No, not much has happened here."

When I went to Raja, their tiny apartment was a sea of humanity. All of them came from the villages. I must tell you that at first I could not find him in their village home. Really, at first I could not find any trace of him there. First there was eviction, then looting and then setting their home on fire. Two of the seventeen women of their (extended) family were missing without their 'wish,' and the Police refused to register in their diary (record). (Muslim) Basanti was the first to tell me about this, but I didn't believe then. Her respected elders said, "It is not that big a deal." There is no surprise that the oppressing males will protect male oppressors. It is like the proverbial, 'All the thieves behave as if they are cousins.' (They are the birds of the same feather.) But in the history of Bengal and the Bengalis this was the first time that a large number of (Hindu) woman were systematically raped at a time when the Prime Minister of the nation was a woman (which is a matter of great pride), and not a single rapist was brought to justice and none was beheaded. It is true that during our 'normal condition' women, both Hindu and Muslim, are being raped in both the Bengals. No society, whether religion-based or democratic, supports rape. There are many religion-based countries in Asia where punishment for rape is beheading.

What I found in Bangladesh was not a riot but a pogrom. Riot means fighting between two groups though they may be unequal: that is taking place in our districts, in colleges, between localities, political parties and among criminals. Riot, most unfortunately, has become order of the day in Pakistan, Yugoslavia, Sri Lanka, Georgia, Azarbaijan, the U. S. and India. Many have written about this in Bangladesh media. In 1992 rioting I saw for myself in (Hindu-majority) Calcutta damaged (Hindu) mandir temples, torched Hindu slums. I also witnessed damaged Muslim mosque and Muslim slums. I have also witnessed such ghastly shameful acts earlier. I have never witnessed that in Bangladesh (non-Muslim) minorities have destroyed (majority Muslim) mosques during rioting, I do not want to see such a thing, and if someone thinks about such criminal acts I would be the first to oppose that.

Both the families knew that I had been in Calcutta few days ago. They enquired about the incidents in detail. Reza's family told me that they had seen the riot-torn pictures of Calcutta and India in T.V. and through videos, and they showed those to me. I had the opportunity to see the misdeeds of the Hindus sitting in Hindu homes there. Moreover, many newspapers and journals printed special issues with pictures of atrocities. But the family said that they never saw any video or news about the riots in their nation, although all the liberal newspapers had written extensively about these atrocities (and about half-a-dozen books were published within a few months). I saw the extreme sad condition of Raja's family. Afterwards I saw video. (In total I saw three videos from three areas of Bangsadesh). In district after district I saw burnt-out villages, businesses, *mandir* temples, ashrams, student-hostels, cremation grounds and endless numbers of homeless people and torched homes. Some members of Raja's family all they did is shed tears. Many have threatened them not to divulge information about these atrocities. It was considered a crime if one said, "I was raped", or "My house is being torched." It was quite amusing when a Bangladeshi-Indian Hindu journalist told me, "It is better not to write about what is happening in

Bangladesh" otherwise he may not be considered secular or intellectual.

Since (1971) Partition our politicians and religious touts have kept the minority population as hostage or *dhimmi*. 'If it happens in India, it will happen here.' This illogic is often mentioned, particularly the bad happenings. Not the good ones. Why no minority, has ever held the posts (like in India) of President, Home Minister, Foreign Minister, head of the United Nation's delegation, ambassador, Vice-Chancellor, Police and Army Chief, bank head (in Bangladesh)? Why not hire (government) sweepers, peon and Prime Minister's Secretary? Why not (as in India) states or self-rule for the minority communities or for the tribal? Why the rate of growth of the Hindu minority community is not higher than the majority? After the latest Bangladeshi pogrom the religion-lovers in India, especially in Calcutta and West Bengal, have been able to do is to say that what happens in Bangladesh (and in Pakistan) may happen here as well. If Pakistan and Bangladesh can become theocratic states, what is wrong if we become such? Pakistan has driven out practically all of her minorities. The majority of Bangladeshi minorities are now living in Indian villages, towns, slums, forests, red-light areas and in pavements. Then what is so wrong if the Indian minorities are driven out (to Pakistan and Bangladesh)? Will we be happy if such things happen? Shall we accept this? At the time of partition the minorities constituted one-third of the population of Bangladesh, and now, according to 2001 census it has come down to only 10%. How are these people vanishing? No one leaves his hearth and home of his forefathers willingly. This matter deserves careful consideration. I extend my best wishes to the couragous journalists, thinkers, writers, intellectuals, politicians, and the social reformers of *back* home.

Chapter 5

Hindu Muslim Bhai Bhai: Hindus and Muslims are Brothers Together

After the 1992 Calcutta Hindu-Muslim riot, to make others believe how much they are non-communal and non-racist people took it upon themselves to write huge graffitis on the walls, or they kept on making such statements. Over and above, all the people were very concerned about happenings in distant Hindi-, Bhojpuri-, Punjabi- or Marathi-speaking worlds, sometimes hundreds, perhaps thousands of miles and many cultural nations away, but they were utterly indifferent about their Bengali homeland of tens of generations. It didn't matter whether they were Communist, rightist, leftist or Naxalite (armed Communist); Congress— Old or New, Janata, Samajbadi (socialist), revolutionary, BJP (Bharatiya Janata) or Muslim League parties. Along with this many were trying to show how anti-religion and atheist they are. Many were talking about Hindu-Muslim brotherhood, and those who believe in religion were attempted to be denigrated. Those who believe in religion their position was clear like water. But time has come to evaluate whether the people who believe in religion are more communal or the followers of Congress or Communist parties. I believe it is easier to fight against overt communalism (racism) than the covert ones. In Africa the anti-apartheid people used to say that. Large number of rulers, oppressors, bureaucrats and intellectuals of West Bengal, Tripura (states) or (of the Federal Indian Government at) Delhi are Bangladeshi-Indian (Hindu or to be precise Bangals or persons of Bangsadeshi origin). If they were truly secular or atheist, Marxist, Socialist or *Gandhi-ite*, as they claim, then why did they leave their homeland? They should have stayed back with their

Muslim and *Namashudra* (oppressed caste) Hindu (vast majority of Hindu population) neighbors. There is only one reason for their leaving their ancestral homeland. Case for refugee Hindu, Buddhist, Christian, including tribal, is altogether different. But, what kind of people are these intellectuals and politicians who left their homeland for fear of their lives? What have they done for their neighbors and relations who stayed back in their homeland believing the age-old saying that 'Mother and motherland are better than paradise'? Why did not they support the Muslim intellectuals (in Bangladesh) who stood by the side of the Hindus? In reality the slogan of our Bangladeshi-Indian Hindus is:

Hindu-Musalman bhai bhai,

(Kintu) tader sangey bash nai.

Hindus and Muslims are brothers together,

(But) they don't live together as neighbor.

But along with this one has to make fiery speeches against communalism. As the Bengalis say, "The mother of a thief defends her son in the loudest voice." It will be a sin to ask these people to go back to live in their home, although these are the people who are always in the forefront in writing and speech making about hidden, covert, discarded racism (communalism). After the 1992-1993 anti-Hindu pogrom in Bangladesh, I myself have visited hundreds of destroyed homes, temples, *smasan* cremation areas, ashrams, libraries, businesses and shops. I have also met ruined women, men and children. I have also witnessed protests around-the-world, except West Bengal (ruled by Bangladeshi Hindus). Are we joining hands with the forces of mass destruction? Is this not a form of communalism (racism)? In the name of salvation are we meditating sitting on lotus pose on top of a corpse (as in ancient Tantrik practices)? Whose corpse is that? Of course not one's own (loved ones). Our ideals are no longer of (the sacrifices of)

Bhagaban (Lord) Krishna, Jesus Christ, (murdered Islamic proponents of) Hassan and Hussein or Gandhiji. Our ideals are not of Dadhichi, the hermit who sacrificed himself so that his strong bones could be used by Lord Indra as devastating weapons to save the Kingdom of God. To stop the killing among Bengali brothers, Mahatma Gandhiji, a non-Bengali from a distant land, an 'outsider,' rushed (in 1946) to Noakhali (during an anti-Hindu pogrom in British India to save Hindus and to bridge Muslim-Hindu divide in Bengal) Gandhi-ites and Calcutta as well. Our Hindu (pacifist) Gandhites to Marxists, from (Hindu) non-believers to believers did just the opposite. Leaving behind the Muslims and poor Hindu of their homeland they ran fast to Hindu India, Hindu West Bengal and Hindu Tripura. These are the people who created Hindustan — Land of the Hindus (the ancient name of India generally credited to Persia), and Hindus West Bengal. Had these people stayed back in their ancestral homeland, would the societies in two Bengals become so racist?

From our mothers and grandmothers we used to hear old folk stories involving cleverness, bluff and deceit. In Hindu/Indian families mothers are the keepers of tradition. These moral stories were told so that we don't do those acts. But it seems that we the Hindu Bengalis have learnt just the opposite. After the (anti-Hindu) pogrom (of 1990) a man from Sylhet (of northeast Bangladesh), now a revolutionary politician of Indian state of West Bengal invited me. I told him that a large number of Hindu families in Sylhet city are spending days in an extremely helpless condition, especially several lowliest of the oppressed-caste poor *Dome* (undertaker) Hindu families living next to the just-destroyed Sylhet city's Jumala Prasad Smasan crematorium. I told him that Apurba babu (Mr. Apurba), Banani devi (Mrs. Banani), and Ram Ram babu (Mr. Ram Ram) were seeking some monetary help to rebuild that cremation complex, including memorials, where many of the fore parents of Mr. Revolutionary were cremated. Near about twenty temples and memorials were destroyed at that *smasan*, the place for sacred cremation was gone. A few years back a chunk of the cremation complex was converted into a (Muslim) burial ground. Mr. Revolutionary's response cannot be quoted here. His statements were quite similar to many of our intellectuals. Many of us cite extremely good reasons for our migration to West Bengal and Tripura (states of India), all of those are, of course, non-communal. For example: Someone's forefather had dreamt of Calcutta, that's why; Some from the town of Cox Bazaar (in the southeast coast of Bangladesh) wanted to live in a big city, that's why he had migrated to Sonamura (a large village in a remote corner of perpetually backward Tripura state in northeast India); or someone so revolutionary that his parents forced him to go to Balurghat (a distant town in northern West Bengal state of India); Some could not return after a vacation in West Bengal with his uncle; Someone else was 'kidnapped' by a bride's family while returning to home to Bangladesh after completing his study in England and decided to stay back at the (rural) Medinipur district; etc. etc.'? Why these people don't treat themselves as Bangladeshi or non-resident Bangladeshi? If after many years the Indians living in Gyana or England (or the United States) can be called 'Indian' or non-resident Indians (N.R.I) then why not the Bengalis whose ancestors have lived at Noakhali or Rajsahi (in Bangladesh) for hundreds of generations are not 'Bangladeshi' or non-resident Bangladeshi (N.R.B.) ? In this respect the anti-Hindu and anti-India 'Bihari' or 'Mojahir' (Muslims who migrated to Pakistan (to create an Islamic nation) are better than us. They do not hesitate that much to be called 'Indian.' And like to visit their *desh* homeland, country of their origin, and do not hesitate to praise or criticize what is good or bad in India.

According to an estimate during the 1992 anti-Hindu pogrom

at least 200,000 Hindus and Buddhists were made homeless, and about 30,000 homes were damaged. In addition to destruction of home, business, (Hindu) mandir, (Buddhist) vihar, (Christian) church, (minority owned) crop-fish farms-cows (domesticated animal resource), many *smasan* cremation areas were also destroyed. A '*malaun*,' the non-believer infidel should not be allowed to give last rites to their loved ones. On that short visit I saw destruction of Tikkar Char *Smasan* of Comilla, the Abhoy Mitra Smasan of Chittagong where both the modern electric crematorium and the traditional wood-based cremation area were gone. Additionally earlier I came across other cremation areas that had been destroyed. Those who are in power at Dhaka, Bangladesh know about this situation very well. Many Muslim writers have criticized these incidents openly, and are doing so now. I enquired of some respected under-taker *Dome* families, from *sadhu* monks and persons belonging to Hindu-Buddhist personalities, if they have any objection to burying their dead. Some of them replied, "even if we do not have any objection the oppressors have." A poor family told me "when we are not even able to bury our dead, then we are forced to do *mukhagni*, touch the secred Eternal Fire on the lips, spread Holy Ganga water on the body and let it float down the river."

Realizing the present socio-economic-political situation in Bengal, once an Arab professor reminded of an Arab proverb, 'if someone is covered with feces and the person finds warmth in that, then he deserves it." If the political leaders and intellectuals get warmth what is there for me to say? But the question remains:- Do the ordinary people deserve this?

Chapter 6
Puja Holydays

In my boyhood days, like other kids, I used to eagerly wait for the annual *Puja* Holiday.[1] The eagerness for Puja Holiday was far greater than for the summer holidays. The climate then is good, moreover during Puja we used to get gifts of new clothing. This was great fun, no doubt. There was *Mahalaya* celebration, a week prior to Durga Puja declaring the beginning of the Holiday season, then there were the sounds of Puja *dhak* drum, visiting of various neighborhood celebrations, unmitigated freedom to wander, watching the deity *Bisarjan* immersion ceremony, joining the *Bisarjan* parade, thereafter *Bijoya* good-wish exchanging festival, visiting homes to receive treats of sweets, *nimki* salted fried pastries, then *kolakuli* embrac of each other, and so much more. Our parents used to say, "Do you know that during our childhood we used to have even more fun. But that fun was different."

We would ask "How come?"

"It used to be our family Puja, it was quite different." We brothers and sisters used to argue at the pitch of our voices, "No,no. We've more fun."

"During Puja holidays we all from faraway places used to get together in one place: our father's brothers *Kaka* and *Jetha* uncles and *Pishi*, father's sister, aunts and their sons and daughters. Once we would gather at the home of *Barir Thakurda*, grandfather at

---

1. In Bengal Puja holiday takes place in autumn covering about three weeks, from the beginning of Durga Puja, welcoming the Mother Goddess Durga to Earth, to the end of Kali Puja of warrior-protector Goddess Kali. *Puja* means offering, worship, meditation, religious service and more.

the home, at other times at the home of *Bar-thakurda*, elder grandpa, and some other year it may be at the *Bhalo-thakurda*, nice grandpa's, or at the *Kala-thakurda*, dark grandpa's." Then he would console us by saying, "You too have fun in Calcutta, but to have so many people under one roof is something else! After the 1947 India-Pakistan Partition neither do you have your native villages and nor do you have your ancestral home. Even if you want, where can you get-together? In the city it is difficult to accommodate so many people at one place. Even before the birds have woken up, we used to go out to pluck flowers; it's a different kind of fun. Then there would be beading of flower garlands, filling up the flower baskets and making flower arrangements on decorative plates."

We would raise our voice and say "Don't you remember? We too used to go out to collect flowers at our Calcutta's Kankulia-*para* (neighborhood). Nay, it was not really plucking flowers, but more like stealing from the homes of uncle Gobindo-*jethamashai*, sister *Kulu-didi*, Mr. *Ganguly-babu*, 'stupid' brother *Bokada*."

At that time almost all the residents of Kankulia were *Bangals* or East-Bengali (Bangladeshi). All of them were Hindu refugee, and renter. There were few exceptions. Only our next-door neighbor Aunt *Kakima* used to go to Barddhamaan district, my friend Bapi's family used to go to Hughly and the ever quarreling Aunt *Khitkhite Pishis* used to go to distant place called either Kanthi or Kandi in the West Bengal state of India. In the middle of that period Kanu *Bangals* of Mymensingh (Bangladesh) were able to build their own two storied house surprising everyone.

When we grew up after Kankulia, I realized that, may be, Ma-Baba were right. We always lived in Calcutta, except on rare occasion someone may have come for a day or two. We rarely went anywhere. Now-a days many people go on holiday travel. At that time neither our parents nor any of our relations had the means to go on holidaying. After school I went to Bengal Engineering College and thereafter to Kharagpur Institute where there were many students who used to go their *desh* village for Puja holiday. Bengalis used to go to their *desh* home in West Bengal's Hooghly, Howrah, Medinipur, Murshidabad, Malda, Jalpaiguri and Assam's Kachar districts, and non-Bengalis to Bihar, Orissa, U.P., Kerala, Andhra and Assam states of India. Occasionally my out-of-town friends used to stay at our Calcutta house to witness 'Puja of Calcutta.' Pujas at Calcutta have glamour, with decorated pandals (marquees), and the lighting. In addition there were delicious *fuchka* (a wafer-ball dipped in tamarind water), *telebhaja* (deep-fired battered vegetable) and cotton-candy; presents of new shirts, trousers, shoes and frocks and saris for girls. Every girl used to look forward to the holiday when they would move up from frock to sari. Long after that I was able to match my parents' description with that of people from their *desh* homeland in Bangladesh. Our friends from Bangladesh visit their *desh* village home at Dhaka, Pirozepur, Sylhet, Chittagong, Kishoregonj, Narsingdi and Gopalgonj during Puja as well as Muslim Id holidays. One may quote the famous Bengali writer S. Wajed Ali, 'That Tradition still Continues.' It is extremely difficult for the dispersed members of extended families to get together under one roof. Now, when we travel from *desh* to *desh*, home to home, I understand that special significance. I still can't remember when all of us — parents, brothers, and sisters, nephews and nieces, got together after 1975. Although only during weddings the entire family meets together, but we cannot stay together, it is not possible. Accommodation is a big problem. Besides, there has been a change in our mindset. Moreover, many family members live in distant cities of Delhi, others at Patna, still others at Pondichery in India or overseas.

Right after our first meeting I developed a close friendship with

Krishna-kanta. Among my close friends he was the one who had homes both at their native village and at the city. Well, it would be wrong to say 'city', it was not a full-fledged city yet. Now it is city. It was a suburb called Kamanapur, little bit open, there were ponds too. Whenever I went to Kamanapur his mother used to treat me very lovingly. As soon as we'd arrive, she'd ask Krishna-kanta, after pulling her sari *ghomta* hood, "Kanta, Why don't you take Sabyasachi to the pond and bring home couple of fish ?" At that time going to Kamanapur needed two bus rides, then after getting down from the bus one had to walk or take a cycle-rickshaw. The other way was to take a train, then walking or a cycle-rickshaw. We mostly walked; it took 15-20 minutes. Later I came to know, and saw, that they had a number of other places in Calcutta. One was at Taltala, where *Barda*, eldest brother, lived. Another was at Ganguli-bagan, where *Fullda*, a middle brother, lived. They may have had another residence at Beleghata, but I never got to go there. It was perhaps mother's younger sister *Chhoto-mashi's*. I've heard a lot about Beleghata from Kanta. Besides these, their extended family members had residences at Kotrang and Barrackpur on the northern suburbs of Calcutta, one on the West Bank; the other on the East Bank of Hughli River. In that extended family others used to live at other places. Kanta's father was a renowned industrialist. For many years they had a factory at Rishra.

Once you approach Kanta's Baokati villlage, one gets a feeling of *bonedi* or aristocracy associated with long tradition. One cannot describe that in words. It is a matter of tradition. It takes time to develop both bad and good traditions. Now I realize that it is associated with the changing patterns of life. Back home they say 'It is because of blood.'

After reaching I was offering unending *pranam* greetings. I was touching elders' feet, they were in turn offering *ashirbad* blessing, 'Baba,[2] let you remain fit,' 'Let you live a thousand years.' Kanta was explaining, "This is uncle *Barro-Jetha*, eldest brother of my father, a physician, from Kathpukur.... Aunt *Barro-Jethima*, wife of *Barro-Jetha*, teaches school, at Kathpukur Ma Annapurna *Uchha-bidyaloi* (high school)..... Youngest uncle *Chhoto-Kaka* teaches physics in Bangabasi College. Stood first in B.A. and M.A.... This is one of the middle uncles *Sejo-kaka*, an engineer at Ranchi in Jharkhand state....Father's sister and her husband, *Pishi* and *Pishey*, both work for the central government in Delhi. Big officers. The older middle uncle, *Mejo-Jetha*, is a renowned lawyer. He practices at the nearby Habibpur district court." Kanta's grandfather is also a reputed lawyer there. I understand that the great-grandfather was also a lawyer there. *Chhoto-dadu*, youngest grandpa, was a physician, and the other *Farsha-dadu*, light-skinned grandpa, is a businessman and owns a launch-service on Kirtankhola River. Two of his uncles and aunts are in politics. "In two parties. One is a rightist and the other a leftist," Kanto confided. "They started politics when they were in college. Now they are quite famous. They've never worked in their lives, even after marriage, and children. They maintained themselves with the earnings from their brothers' earnings. There was no deprived living, but luxurious life of the Europeans. Afterwards wealth came through the parties." I heard one of them became a minister. To be honest it was very difficult to discern who was the son or daughter of which uncle or which aunt. Among his father's immediate brothers and sisters someone used to be in politics too.

Baokati village was so near, yet so far. Although the distance was no more than 70-75 miles, it used to take almost half-a-day to reach. By train, bus, ferry on Chhoto (small) Kirtankhola River, and then on foot. Or, by train, then a three-wheeler *tempo* van

2. An affectionate term for younger male, also means father.

instead of bus, ferry, then cycle rickshaw instead of walking. Now-a days one can take three-wheeler auto (scooter taxis) instead of bus. But then one has to get off at Jagatballavpur. On another route one may go via Sripur after Siakhola. Then by bus and walking, it adds up another one to one and one-half hours. This is the root you've to take if you go by car. There is national highway up to Siakhala, then a paved road for Jaleswar, on way is Baokati. The road up to Jaleswar is beautiful. It was built during the zamindari[3] era, lined with trees on both sides.

Once you walk ahead from the *ghat*, the steps to the water and the ferry dock, you'll see the main *singha-darja*, lion-statue entrance. A little to the front stands their two-storied rural-type large *dalan-bari* house. There is a verandah in the front and upstairs too. If you turn right there stands their two-storied *kachhari-bari* office building. There are people all the time, even during Puja holidays. Adjacent to that is a small one-storied *Daktar-bari*, physician (medical) building. On your left is the huge Puja *mandap,* raised platform, where the Puja is held. Between the big building and the medical building, there is a pond, and behind the Puja *mandap*, there is a lake. Both sides are flanked by gardens; on the side and back there is paddy field, besides there are additional ponds, cow-shed, and so much more.

In the midst of joy, something bothered me because I couldn't find *Borrda* and *Fullda*, older brothers. Kanta and I used to sleep in the same room. At the dawn I heard Aunt *Mashima*, Kanta's mother raised him from bed, then took him over to the verandah, and whispered him, "Did you visit *Barda*? When did you go to Taltala? Did you hand over the new shirt and sari to them? I hope you didn't show those to anyone in the house. Did Dipali say anything? When did you go to Ganguli-*bagan*? Did *Fullda* like the shirt? Are they able to manage with that income?

---

3. Pre-British and early-British, from middle of last millennium.

Does the house belong to a friend of Sylheti-*kaka*, uncle from Sylhet (Bangladesh)? And many more questions. In sleepy eyes Kanta just answered, "Yes," "No," "Fine," "All right ," etc. They 'conversed' for some time. For Aunt *Mashima* living in an extended family, that may been the only personal time with her son. Because of me, Kanta was never alone. My guess is that *Mashima* may have been weeping at times. Her mental condition was such that she did not care whether I was sleeping or not. After his conversation Kanta lied next to me again. Facing the other side, he uttered in soft voice, "Don't say it to any one. I'll tell you later." The way he said it was sure that I was awake, and I have heard the private conversations of mother and son. He must have understood that I was faking sleep.

After the *Bisarjan* immersion ceremony, *Bijoya* greetings and *kolahuli* hugging, blessings, sweet eating, Kanto and I left for Calcutta on *Ekadashi*, the eleventh day of the moon. After 20 minute of the Chhoto Kirtankhola River, we took the bus. We found seats next to each other. 40 minute journey. Kanto breathed a sigh of relief, as if he was holding it. "Do you know why *Barda* and *Fullda* did not come? They are prohibited to come. Dad at his older brother Jetha's order has asked them not to come. We are not allowed to keep any relation with them. Because of this my father's younger brother and his wife, *Chhoto-Kaka* and *Kakima*, and Ma had serious altercation with Dad and his older brother and his wife *Jetha* and *Jethima*. This spread to other uncles and aunts too. For a time, they almost stopped talking to each other. It is a bit normal now." Kanto continued with a pause, "Borrda's sin was that he proposed to marry his classmate Dipali. Hearing this, *Jetha* and *Jethima* were enraged. Supposedly Dipalidi, Dipali older sister, belongs to a different caste. Our seven-generations will become impure! We will be outcasted. *Chhoto-kakima*, younger aunt, and Ma said 'You guys eat that caste.' We don't need that garbage."

"Mejo-Pishi and Pishey, father's middle sister and her husband, said 'This pride in caste will destroy you all.' Still Baba and *Jetha* Uncle did not budge. Dipalidi hails from a famous family. She topped in the exams, and studied together. Her parents are very nice. And highly educated. At last, the wedding and the *Boubhat*, groom's family reception, were both held at Dipalidi's house. Mother gave me money to buy wedding gifts of bride's sari, *dhuti* and *punjabi* shirt for the groom. Jhantu, Tapas, Dipak, Raja, Nayan, Sabya, Sontu and I accompanied the groom as *Barjatri*, groom's courtiers. Except for Ma and Aunt Kakima, no one knows this. *Barda* has been disowned. And *Fulda*. So that youngsters do not dare to marry out-of-caste.

"And Fullda wanted to marry Pranatidi, older sister Pranati. They're Brahmo by religion. So he is also barred from coming here, even during the Puja. *Fulda* is going through a big financial crisis. Thank God *Barda* was there. Mother secretly sends money through me. They will get married in the next year, after *Fulda* gets a job. What is funny is that both Pranatidi's and we have the same last name. They are more aristocratic, *bonedi*, than us. And hail from a better family. Joida of Kotrang has a different problem. His wife, sister-in-law *Pari-baudi*'s family is Muslim, but *Paribaudi* is Hindu. She is an Engineer from B.E. College. Her father Dr. Enayet Khan is a renowned engineer. *Pari-boudi*'s formal name is Raosan Khan Sarkar, but everybody calls her as Pari, the Fairy. *Pari-baudi*'s mother Aunt *Hasi-mashi* was Hindu too, and was engaged daily with Hindu *puja* service and with other routine *Ekadashi, Sankranti* rituals and festivals. Always wore Hindu wedding *sankha* conch bracelets and *sindur* vermillion mark on the scalp. Aunt *Hasi-mashi* raised *Pari-boudi* as a Hindu. Uncle *Khan-mesho* always wears traditional outfit of *dhuti* and Bengali *punjabi, fotua* or *neema* shirts during all the Hindu puja festivals, and during *Ekadashi, Sankranti* festivities. But my father and elder uncles are all *sahibs* (Western or anti-Hindu). We've heard that during Partition at their Tangail, near Dhaka, homeland Muslim *goondas* (thugs) after killing her elder and middle brothers took the girls as bounty. After *Hashi-mashi's* release when she returned home, her father and uncles didn't want to take her back as she was *nashta* or desecrated. Her mother may have committed suicide for this. My Aunt Kakima used to say, "Can you tell me, Are Hindus human? Is there any flesh and blood in their body? Do they have soul? What about kindness, affection and pity? Intelligence, brain?" She used to say, "Her father and uncles were incompetent in protecting her. Once she came back alive, instead of them offering her celebratory garlands, asking her for forgiveness, and worshipping her through puja, they turned her away? They were demons, worst than animal. There will not be any room for them in the Hell either."

When no Hindu family agreed to give *Hashi-mashi* a shelter Mr. Enayet's family offered shelter to Hashi. After giving her college education, Enayet's Mother offered this marriage proposal. She first wrote to Hasi's family if they had any suggestion for a Hindu groom. Hasi's family did not even have the courtesy to reply. But after their marriage there were pressure from the Muslim priest *Mullah*, relations, neighbors, headmen for Muslim conversion of Hashi. One day some *goondas* (thugs) appeared with iron rods and sticks. They wanted Hashi to read Islamic *kalma* conversion oath immediately. Somehow the couple was able to seek a little time, and in the middle of the night sought good-bye from his parents, and at first went to Dhaka, now Bangladesh, then to Calcutta, India. After wandering from place to place, they finally settled at Tumchar village, next to Baokati. Even in the 1980s, one of my acquaintances, Mr. Nagen Ghosh of Noakhali, Bangladesh had to flee with his married Muslim wife Nazmun as they were hounded by Muslims. Their demand? Nagen must be converted to Islam. And just a few years back Bishnu Sutradhar, a Hindu, had to flee to America with his Muslim wife Lutfunnnesa Chapala, as the Islamist thugs demanded Bishnu's conversion. His house at Kishoregonj was set on fire by the Islamists. Still a few years later rest of the family members were living as refugee at Bagura in the north at his middle brother's house.

Four years ago when I was visiting Mr. Barun's Puja at his ancestral village at Tangail in Bangladesh, I landed in a very uneasy situation. I was going to Barun's village, but Barun wasn't joining. The reason was the same, but possibly the real reason was the hurting of the feelings of the family elders by choosing one's partner than one initiated by the elders of two families. Barun married a Hindu out-of-caste, and if they went as if the entire Puja celebration would be maligned. I said to myself, I don't need to maintain any relationship with that kind of purity. I did not know this beforehand. As I was about to leave, I learned. Barun and his wife Papri requested with folded hands "Dada, older brother, for our sake, please do not cancel the trip. A big commotion has begun hearing that you may cancel the trip. Please save our face." Even after so much misery and oppresion, so many Hindu minds haven't changed, after decades of Hasi-Enayet's experience. It reminds me of the cases of barbaric oppression in 1971 of Bengali girls in Dr. Nilima Ibrahim's book, *Birangana*, by the Islamist Pakistanis. As the primary target of the Pakistanis and Bengali Islamists were Hindus (and Muslim secular and pro-independence individuals), as a result disproportionate majority of the victims were Hindu. No Hindu father, uncle or grandfather was able to protect their daughters and wives, but none of them, according to their nature, in Dr. Nilima Ibrahim's book, had courage and backbone to take the victims back. "I believe, most Hindus have had no perceptible change in their cruel, unhealthy, inhuman characteristics," said a critic.

"Everybody would say that no one could guess from Pari-boudi's mannerism that she was from a Muslim family. Her marriage was held according to Hindu custom. Pari-boudi's father and Aunt Kanto Pishi arranged for a Hindu priest. *Pari-baudi* always wears Hindu *sankha* conch-bangles and vermilion *sindur* mark. Still my father and *Jetha* uncle wouldn't change their mind. They won't even accept water from her. She is an outcaste, of a different religion. Since that time, as a protest, Mr. Bijoy Dutta, a pious Hindu, doesn't take water from my father and elder Jetha uncle. Mother, *Kaka* Uncle and *Kakima* Aunt used to visit our brothers telling others that they are going to Tarakeswar, a place of pilgrimage. And did everything with them. They would say to my Baba and Jetha, 'We don't need that kind of water from you.'

Observing the meanness of our elders, Ma, *Kaka* and *Kakima* used to say that "it won't be long for the family to become heirless. Everyone's bad, except themselves, all are disposable. All are invisible, untouchable. How can someone who is narrow-minded, who has nothing to offer and suffers from inferiority complex welcome others as their own? They cannot make others as part of thier own." They also used to say, "Such people cannot think others as human. They do not think themselves complete unless they are able to create division among them. They blame the proselytizers for conversion but cannot convert anybody into their own religion. They would not accept water from other; if married outside then they'd outcaste. And they in the name of casteism and purity drive others from Hinduism. For them it is a sin if one converts to Islam or Christianity, and even if mixed families remain Hindu nobody should propose marriage with their sons and daughters. Thank goodness that they are a minority!"

Kanto said, his mother used to say "Our people will be finished for their false pride in caste. Everything will be finished for us." Then she would add, "Your Uncle *Chhoto-Kaka* used to say remorsefully, that some people say that in the Holy Scripture

Bhagaban, God, said that He/She has created four castes. First of all, he used to say that, no one has suggested that all Hindus have to follow that scripture. More importantly where has it been said that one gets caste on the basis of birth? Only on the basis of sex? And if that were true then one may obtain caste by selling one's body! Moreover where's the discussion of high and low? Significantly that description was on the basis of work, meaning the division of labor. Man and woman would receive caste on the basis of deed and knowladge; not because of union between man and woman, through intelligence; and through knowledge, work, and education."

But then again looking at Salam, a Muslim, in America one becomes skeptical. I have seen him as a prejudice-free liberated person. A fresh Ph.D. Dr. Nilima Bhattacharya, a Hindu, fell in love with him. As soon as she fell in love, Salam and his mother, my *Tanji-baudi*, Tanji sister-in-law, started teaching her Muslim *Namaz* prayer, Islamic conversion scripture, Arabic, keeping of *Roza* fasting, skipping Bengali sari for Arabic dress, and forcing Nilima to eat cow flesh, anathema to Hindus, day and night. *Tanji-baudis* were Hindus just three generations ago. Salam was a good student, yet had weakness for wine and women, prohibited in Islam. I didn't know that he even knew something called *Namaz*. My Muslim friend Mansur said, "I asked Salam, 'Mia,[4] what's the matter? He replied, 'Forget about Hindu culture. That kind of *Nomo*[5] foreign culture Khadeja must change. I have given Nilima a new name Khadeja Begum after making her read *Kalma* prayer for Islamic conversion.'" I read somewhere 'A Devil does not need any pretense.' And what about Nilima's thesis on women's liberation?"

For decades I could not go home during Durga Puja. Within

---

4. An invocation for Muslims in Bengal.
5. A derogatory term for Hindus.

hours of my arrival home, I got a call from Kanta, "Are you coming?"

"Where?"

"Where else? To *desh*, village. Have you forgotten all about Puja at our village? You have been there many times."

"No, how can I forget? I came here just for a few days. I haven't watched Puja in a long time, that's why I was thinking of not leaving Calcutta this time."

"How can that be? Come at least for a day. Shuvo, Joyeeta and Shefali will enjoy it, especially U.S.-born Shuvo and Joyeeta who had never watched Puja festivities in Bengal. They never watched Puja at home village."

"That's true."

"It will be for half-a day. I too will be there for only half-a-day. There is not much splendor any more. It takes only a short time these days. We'll start early in the morning then we will be back late evening."

The entire party was there early morning before the start of the morning puja service of *Nabami* (or *Navami*, the fourth day of) celebration of Durga Puja.[6] But what was I seeing? I could not believe my eyes. There were hardly any people, no crowd. Just a few elderly people were hanging around. As I was going to touch the feet of Aunt Mashima (Kanta's mother), she pulled me and broke down in tears, "Sachi, they've finally been able to drive everyone away. None of our children's families come here anymore. You already know about Kanto's elder brothers Barda, Fulda, and younger maternal Aunt *Chhoto-mashi*. One by one

---

6. Durga Puja of the Mother Goddess is celebrated for five days, from *Sashti* — sixth day of the moon, to *Bijoya Dasami* — tenth day of the moon, when the sculptures of the deity are immersed into rivers or lakes for *Bisarjan* festivity for new life to begin.

others have left home as well. You too are here for part of a day."
While giving updates for the past decades she said, "This casteism
has destroyed Hindus. No one is acceptable from *Bhagaban*
(Lord) Buddha and Mahabir to Sri Chaitanya, Rammohun,
Vidyasagar and Vivekananda.[7] They all are untouchable. We are
finished. You are like my own child Kanto; I can tell you my intimate
family story."

While talking she used to take a deep breath and say to herself,

Once Puja holidays are over

O Mother take me into arms of your's.[8]

After the mid-day *Bhog*, sacred food for lunch, Mrs. Ananya
Kirtaniya, singer of devotional *Kirtan* songs, and Mr. Kartik
Baul,[9] singer of *Baul* folk songs, were invited to perform for us.
Kartick sang a *Baul* song of Lalan Fakir;[10]

Sob lokey koi Lalon ki jat aei sangsarey,

Everyone's asking, what's Lalon's family caste?

Lalon says, in my life no one has figured that out.

---

7. Buddha is the founder of Buddhism, Mahavir of Jainism, both of 6th
   century B.C., Sri Chaitanya, 15th century popularized anti-caste
   Vaishnav pacifist movement, Rammohun, 19th century founder of
   monotheistic Brahmoism, Vidyasagar and Vivekananda, both 19th
   century notables, all of whom reformed Hinduism.
8. In traditional Hindu belief one goes back to the bosoms of Mother
   Earth.
9. *Bauls* are Bengal's wandering singing minstrels, they are traditionally
   "a class of Hindu stoical devotees singing songs in a special mode
   illustrating their doctrine" *Bauls* have been coming from all religious
   groups, often claiming all of them.
10. 18th-19th century. Lalon was a *Fakir* or Muslim mendicant ascetic,
    a singer, composer and song writer, born to a Hindu family but was
    raised by a Muslim, and claimed both as his own.

Circumcision makes a Muslim a man, what's proscribed for woman?

Sacred thread recognizes Brahmin man, how do you know a Brahmin woman?

Some wear (Hindu) *mala* garland, others *tasbi* (Muslim) beads,

Do those make different kin?

At the time of birth and death, what's left of a face?

Nonsense talk of race, we quarrel all over the face.

Lalan says this talk about 'r caste drowned our pleasure real fast.

After that song Ananya Kirtaniya started a *Kirtan,*

The brother who seeks division in this life

Can't meet Krishna, says his friends and their wives.

What is the difference between a slayer and a priest?

They had no say in their birth and end.

(Krishna says) men 'n women, they're all my chidren.

(Those who) think of high-n-low, will find even Hell is forbidden.

Chapter 7

In the Land of the Goddess

Worship of the Goddess of Power (Strength) or *Shakti Puja* has made a special place in the life of the Bengalis. Of late *Durga Puja*, worshipping the Mother Goddess, has become its prime manifestation. During the past 200 to 300 years lots of modifications and enhancements have taken place of that celebration. As a result there has been improvements to its presentation and decoration, and development in the related traditional, rural and cottage industries. Over and above this puja celebration has transformed itself from the patronage of individual families to community celebrations. Because of receiving community support, distances in Hindu Bengali society on the basis of caste, creed, race, and wealth have been reduced, although I feel we will have to go a long way to further reduce the narrow-mindedness. This essay aims at highlighting our narrow mindedness and its contradictions that we suffer from.

Bengalis have had a long connection with *Shakti Puja* worship through Goddess Ma Kali, the destroyer of the Demons and the protector of her earthly children. Although in the ancient Hindu *Purana* literature there are many discussions of the meaning of Ma Kali, among the Hindu traditions, the Bengali Hindus came to be associated closely with Mother Kali through *Shakti Puja* or seeking physical strength. That is why in every nook and corner of Bengal one finds *mandirs* (temples) to Goddesses Kali, Bhavani, Chandi and in many of Her incarnations. Out of all of these, the Kali *Mandir* temple at Ramna in Dhaka is perhaps the oldest. It is about a thousand year old. We also learn from (Muslim) Professor Abdul Jabbar's book that from this temple locality the Bengalis beloging to all faiths and sects used unite to fight against (Muslim) Isha Khan (in the Middle Age). The genocidal anti-

Hindu regime of Pakistan Government demolished this temple and the adjacent ashram of Ma Anandamoyee during the independence war of Bangladesh (1971). Along with the *Mandir* it tried to destroy the entire Hindu society, and make Muslim Bangladeshis communal anti-infidel. The first Bangladesh Gavernment, a pro-secular regime, instead of rebuilding this, completed the destruction. Many individuals have tried to rebuild them, among them is our respected Aunt *Mashima* (mother's sister), Mrs. K. B. Roy-Chowdhury. She told me that she herself met *Bangabandhu* (Father of the Nation, President Mujibur Rahman) and General Zia (President Zia ur Rahman), and appealed them for reconstruction. I firmly believe that Bengali's like Mashisma will be able to restart *Shakti Puja* celebration at Ramna. Just as Buddha Puja, worshipping of Lord Buddha is a popular festival among Bengali Hindus, so is *Shakti Puja* has become a part of the Tibetan Buddhism through the worship of Goddess Kali as Mahakal Puja. Sometime back I was invited by a Buddhist *Lama* priest for a *Darshan* glimpse of the Goddess Kali at a Mahakal temple at Ladakh or Little Tibet in India. "Donation Box" had a sign in Bengali as well.

But being devotees of Shakti or power, have we become powerful men and women? Or, have we become morbid and impotent? Likewise, in recent times large number of (Bengali) individuals like Sri Chaitanya (15th century), Sri Ramakrishna (19th century), (19th-20th century) Swami Vivekananda and Swami Pranavananda (founder of Bharat Sevashram Sangha), the founder of Krishna conscious movement, ISKON, Sri Prabhupad and many sages, hermits and housewives have spoken up against caste, creed and gender discrimination. Are we paying any attention? But, any result? We are energetically contradicting each other. This is true that many Bangladeshi Hindus (and Buddhists and Christians) are becoming victims of narrow-mindedness of some in the majority Muslims and by anti-Hindu community. In Bangladesh many Hindus, Muslims, Buddhists and Christians have written about this. I too have written on the issue. We need to think whether we are becoming victims ourselves, and must think about the gravity of our action.

I was reminded of this issue at the discourse of Gita Sangha at a Hindu community of Dhaka on Thursday 16th July, 1998, and in the discourse of Mahanagar (metropolitan) Puja Committee on Friday, 17th July at Dhakeswari Mandir temple, someone raised these unpleasant truths about our self-contradictions. Similar issues were raised at a lecture on *Janmastami* (Lord Krishna's birthday) celebration on Saturday, 15th August 1998 at New York.

The Riddle of Caste:

Side-by-side with the dedication to *Shakti*, a cult-like devotion for *Shanti* (peace) and non-violence had been a part of Bengali life for a long time. The spread of *Vaishnavism* is the result of this. The arrival of Sri Chaitanya in the Middle Age had not only helped the Bengali Hindu society to liberate itself from social ills, but also helped rejuvenate entire Bengal, Hindu and Muslim. For this reason the advent of Sri Chaitanya was a revolutionary event. By giving love, he created a tidal wave of love. The attackers and tyrants instead of defeating him, lost to Sri Chaitanya. He came to spread his message by saying, "Just because you have hit me, am I not going to give you love?" Some say this is the true example of a 'revolutionary pacifist' or 'militant pacifism.' Like the proverbial, *sonar pathar baati*, 'golden stone bowl,' it is true. In the 20th century Gandhiji followed the same path. At Chaitanaya's call the privileged and the oppressed caste, *Chandal*, oppressed of the oppressed castes, and Brahmin, privileged caste, Hindus, followers of Shakti and Shiva traditions and Muslims were initiated into pacifist Vaishnavism. Thus became the tradition of 'To God everyone is a servant, male or female, *das* or *dasi*.' He also showed

the path of women's emancipation. After his demise we started
our downhill journey. Forgetting about not only bringing others to
our pacifist fold, but it also became routine for people to be driven
out of one's own Hindu faith. Again birth became a primary
criterion for attaining status, not work (knowledge). That day a
speaker at Dhaka reminded us from the Holy Gita, God says,
"*Chaturbarnang Maya Shristang Gunakarma Bidhagasha*"
(3:18), meaning "I have created four castes according to character
and deed" (see, *Gita* edited by Jagadish Ghosh). No where was
it said (man-made) caste was hereditary. In India, there is a saying
'One becomes *brahmin* through knowledge and deed, not by
birth.' Though we parrot it we do not follow that. The result has
been our backwardness, so-called rivalry between high and low,
the rise of prejudice, the rise of the intolerance, oppression of
women, ousting from society, and religious negativism.

Bengal's Emancipation of Women :

In our Hindu society alongside the reformation of religion and
society exists conservatism. There exist liberal thinking; next to it
are narrow-mindedness and inferiority complex. For thousands
of years Hindus have preached for equal status of men and women,
and this has resulted in the rise of powerful goddesses. Alas in
that society there is oppression of women, torture, violation of
their modesty! Now-a days any parent knows what one goes
through to have the *kanya-ratna*, girl-jewel, married off. Sadly
though the gem-like *putra-ratna*, son-jewel, needs no effort for
marrying off, and realize how much our goddesses are worth. I
have written this extensively in the *Kapurush* (Coward) chapter
of my book, *A Aamar Desh* (This is my country, College Street
Publishers, Calcutta, 1998), so I won't dwell on it further. If we
want to develop our society, if we want to stop its decline, then
the majority of the nation, women, who constitute 51% of our
population, must have equal status, as well as other oppressed

non-privileged castes who constitute 80% of Indian population. On one hand we would worship the Mother and on the other we would disrespect and neglect Her. Can this go together? On one hand we would worship Goddesses Durga, Kali, Saraswati, Lakshmi and Manasha,[1] on the other hand we would accept bribe in the name of dowry during weddings, Are these devotion or insult to the Goddesses? We must think when we are oppressed by others, if we ourselves have opened the door of such torture by our own action of oppression at home. In this context I remember the book, *Aami Birangana Bolchhi* (I, a courageous woman speaking, Jagriti, Dhaka, 1998) written by respected author Dr Nilima Ibrahim, a Hindu by birth and married to a Muslim. This book lists cases of girls and women who were abused by the Pakistani army and Bengali Islamists. But it was regrettable that my Hindu relatives or neighbors could not take back their girls. (The conditions of rehabilitation of Muslim girls were not that bad). We, the fathers, uncles, brothers, were incapable of protecting our girls, moreover we transferred our incompetence on our daughters and wives. We failed to kill the *Asur* demon like Ma Durga, and failed to give assurance (from Demons after killing them) like Goddess Kali. Society does not stand still. Some changes have taken place as societal reformation. We know many individuals who are enjoying their lives after marrying into other castes and religions. I know some religious Hindu families whose names are (Muslim) Rahman, Rahamatullah, Asgar, Shovan, and (Christian) Thomas, Gomez and many other traditionally non-Hindu names.

Shakti Devotion and Demon Killing:

We have been told through our festivities to fight injustice with the help of truth. Killing of Demons have been encouraged to

---

1. Goddesses of strength, protection, learning, wealth and snake (wild animals) respectively.

bring peace to our society, but not by giving up on our country, society, family and sons and daughters. Goddess Durga went to war taking her sons and daughters. In the *Bhagabat Gita* Lord Krishna reminded Arjun (the fighter who refused to kill his enemy relations and gurus):

Time I am, the great destroyer of the worlds, and I have come here to destroy all people. With the exception of you (the Pandavas), all the soldiers here on both sides will be slain.

In spite of this, when Arjun was not inclined to fight, the Lord said:

Therefore get up. Prepare to fight and win glory. Conquer your enemies and enjoy a flourishing kingdom. They are already put to death by My arrangement, and you, O Sabyasachi, can be but an instrument in the fight.

But in spite of reading Gita and worshipping the Demon-killing Durga, how many times have we tried to fight against crime, torture and oppression? Or, did we try to flee as soon as we hear of torture and oppression? We must think why has this happened and is still happening. God asked us to take up arms even against one's own family, and even against the gurus to fight injustice. Still, we must think, why have we become lifeless, spineless, escapists believing in running away? Of late a number of smart, intelligent, and powerful women and men like Mother Durga have appeared. I firmly believe if we help them they will be able to suppress our *Asur* Demons.

6

Chapter 8
The Other Side of Rapture

This essay is the result of numerous visits to Bangladesh-West Bengal partitioned borders and my assessment of the changes in societies in both the Bengals. This also follows from my experience with the Bengalis, Bangladeshis and Indians, in a foreign country, and attending conferences with Indian and Bangladeshi Bengalis including academic Bengal Studies Conferences. Associated with that I have included the nostalgia of the *Bangals*, the East Bangali Hindu refugees and their descendants living in India about the images of thier *desh*-homeland they left behind.

In fact many in West Bengal and India have good and correct idea of East Bengal, now Bangladesh. Side by side West Bengalis (Indian Bengalis) have nurtured many unreal, distorted, truth-evading ideas for all of the past 50 years. I am becoming more convinced about this as my family and I travel across the partitioned border, as I am learning about it from reading newspapers and magazines, and socializing with the people there. In addition, the images of Bangladesh that have been created in West Bengal through the book with titles like, 'The *desh* homeland we've left behind,' or emotionally fictitious, 'Bengal of the Other Side'. This essay is about the perception and reality of the 'other side' for the people living on the other side. My Bangladeshi family was connected with Calcutta, then the capital of the united Bengal provnice and for a long time capital of British India, long before 1947 partition. But we were always *Bangal* or East Bengali to my relatives, friends and neighbors. From my father's side our ancestral homeland is Barisal district and my mother's at Faridpur. Our last name is identified regionally with Barisal. But my parents' final migration to Calcutta was the result of partition. Otherwise they might have come to Calcutta for schooling, but they would have had connections with their native village like the migrants from states of Bihar, Orissa, Assam, Nepal, other parts of West Bengal to Calcutta and as the natives of Bangladesh districts who migrate to Dhaka, the capital, for work.

We all have created myths about Bangladesh and West Bengal across the borders. We've created absurd fairy-tales, and this essay is to highlight a few of those. There is a great deal of difference between myth and reality, and even after Bangladesh was born, when exchanges were possible, the difference still persists. Some say it has widened. In some areas the difference is as wide as heaven and hell. I have grown up with this myth, and many of my relatives and friends living in (Bengali-majority Indian) West Bengal and Tripura states pretend they still believe in them. The more I know, more I learn, and the more I see, I believe that it is wrong to perpetuate wrong myths; it is harmful for both the nations, and with it is connected the relations between Bengali and other peoples in the Subcontinent. As a result have suffered, and are still suffering, the Bangladeshi Hindu minorities, and minorities of both sides. Against this backdrop, it is criminal to try to perpetuate false myths. This illusory situation has developed because of our failure to distinguish between our personal experience and communal or group relation. Added to this is *Bhadrolok's*, gentlemen's, inability to tell the unpleasant truth.

The Bangladeshis of Indian origin and others have also created new myths about West Bengal, but that is not the main focus of my writing. For politics in India all the political parties, nationalists, Congress, Communist, the non-Communist Left, pro-Hindu and pro-Islam groups, have nurtured it, and are still keeping it alive. Before 1947 partition Congress Party came to be known as a non-secular Hindu Party to some middle-class Muslims in East

Bengal, as a result it was difficult for Congress to challenge the larger Muslim society. The leftists did not have that problem as they supported Muslim League's demand for Muslim-Hindu India partition. Left never tried to confront these myths hurting both nations. Of late few journalists from Calcutta have been making critical analysis, going beyond their euphoria. But their numbers are too small.

Most are aware of the fact that a large section of Bangladeshi (Muslim) intellectuals hold Hindu Bengali, Right and Left, responsible for the partition of Bengal and India, whereas in West Bengal and in India, the Muslim League Party and Muslim separatism are held responsible for partition. We all know that since the first partition of Bengal in 1905, Hindu-Muslim killing became a part of then united Bengal, which resulted in the 'Great Calcutta Killing' of 1946 during British colonial rule. Afterwards in the Noakhali mass killing (pogrom) about 7,000 Hindus were killed. Thereafter since 1947 partition, almost every year there has been anti-Hindu pogroms in Bangladesh for which strangely the Congress and the Communists of West Bengal run by Bangladeshi Hindu refugees, and India held each other responsible. With this started the game of politicking with the hapless Hindu refugees in West Bengal, Tripura and India. How many of us and which party ever condemned this killing? We created trouble elsewhere. As we never protested these killing of Hindus either in Hindu refugee-run West Bengal or in Muslim-run Bangladesh, very few Bangladeshis, even progressives, know of the immense loss, especially how tragically the Bangla minorities have been suffering due to partition. One of my Bangla professor friends told me, "You know, once I wrote that because of 1947 Partition, lots of people have suffered," the editor returned back my article and said, "Don't write those, very few people in the nation believe that." I got the same response from many when asked. A small number of people, Muslim and non-Muslim, in Bangladesh have raised this issue, yet even fewer in refugee-run, Communist-ruled Indian states of West Bengal and Tripura. Lately there have been a few activists and scholars who have spoken up in faraway nations.

When asked the intellectuals and politicians of Calcutta of their deafening silence about their Bangladesh, especially about condoning oppression of their own family in Bangladesh, they cite two reasons. One, about their non-interference in the affairs of other nations and in other states of India, and secondly, "It will have adverse effect on Hindus." But, how worse could that have been after the direct displacement of over thirty million people (over forty-five million including the descendants), killing of about three million Hindus, then there were refugee camps, Sealdah Station, Dandakaranya, Andaman[1] and deaths due to disease and starvation? But, the socialist-influenced egalitarianism, Communist atheist-influenced support for the downtrodden, and nationalist-influenced pride in one's root, West Bengalis never hesitated to protest against any, foreign or domestic, oppression around-the world: from Kashmir to Kerala, Punjab to Pondicherry, North America or South Africa, from Palestine to Poland, yet not his own *desh* homeland? I do not know yet if this is due to the self-centeredness of the Hindu mind, or fatalism of Hindu religion, or due to a new kind of racism.

---

1 All over West Bengal, Tripura, Assam and Bihar states of India there were refugee camps for Bengali Hindu refugees. Sealdah Station was one of the terminals in Calcutta where perennially lived new sets of refugee families many of whom are present-day educated Calcuttans, who fled to India (illegally) by train, but had nowhere to go. In Dandakaranya Forest in Central India and Andaman Islands in the Bay of Bengal new refugee settlements were started by the federal Delhi Government after a large-scale Hindu killing and displacement in the 1960s.

Many Bangladeshi Muslims suggest that there were no anti-Hindu 'riot' killings, and if there were any, those must have been initiated by Hindus themselves. But, when asked our refugee families and friends, and even Bangladeshi Hindus, Buddhists and Christians, narrate in minute details the dates of pogroms, the rise tension, and the events of terror. And the reasons when they were 'forced' to leave their ancestral homeland. Many Bangladeshis have told me that they personally know when Hindu neighbors were given shelter by Muslims. Or, they know when families met catastrophe, or they know when religious institutions were destroyed or desecrated, or someone had to change one's religion. Yet they cannot fathom when the situation became 'normal' why that family left their homeland. Many of them look for excuse elsewhere, in some unreal abstract reason: 'Leader of that locality,' 'Thug from that neighborhood,' 'Head officer of that Police Station,' 'That District Administrator's brother-in-law.' The only problem is not the anti-Hindu pogroms there. The sufferers in Bangladesh think that it is also a problem of Bengali Hindu intellectuals of West Bengal, India, whose lion's share happens to be Bangladeshi Hindu or *Bangal*. Many have asked, Why is it that our intelle tuals who are engaged in demonstration and eloquent writ ng about minority oppression in America, Great Britain, Northern Ireland, Palestine, or South Africa, but remain dead silent on Bangladesh? During my student life, I have attended many such processions and demonstrations in Calcutta. Is it because of this hypocrisy and double-standard that many Bangladeshis call them 'Hindu Marxist' or 'Hindu Atheist.' It reminds me of Mr. Subodh, a Hindu, of Barisal, Bangladesh, whom I met in 1982 and in 1995. He said, "In 1994 I've sent my youngest son Sujit to Calcutta. He is a brilliant student. Went to college here for a year. Now he lives in Barasat, a border town in West Bengal. He's really interested in Marxism! as if there is no need for Marxism or socialism in Bangladesh. But what actually happened was narrated by Ramkamal, a Hindu, and Muksud, a Muslim. A local Muslim leader had moved into their home, through the abuse of Enemy Property Act by declaring that homesteads of patriotic Hindus as 'enemy property.' And the occupier had warned them then not to complain. Subodh was afraid if he had complained, harm may come to Sujit. Father and son didn't protest against that oppression. Soon Sujit became a spokesman for the 'Palestine land grab by the Israelis.' According to my friend Professor Mohammad Faisal's theory, although Hindus went to India as a persecuted minorrity, but the psyche of their power-grabbing middleclass were that of colonialists where they have been able to establish their colonial rule in India, almost like the Spanish and Portuguese of South and Central America, the English and the French in North America, Caribbean and Australia. Initially in Pakistan too the Urdu speaking North Indian Muslims, *Mojahirs*, the pious migrants, controlled the state power. The only goal of our Bangladeshi Hindu elites, intellectuals and politicians was to capture power in West Bengal and Tripura by encouraging Bangladeshi Hindus to come to India thereby increasing their vote-bank. Had they protested and reduced oppression it might have lowered migration. On this issue, the Hindu Bengali rulers are still maintaining that double-standard. Because of persecution, over 40,000 mostly-Buddhist Chakma tribes fled from Bangladesh hills and were living in 'camps' in Tripura. They were driven out of Chittagong Hill Tracts of Bangladesh and living under indescribable hardship. The Bengali Communist-Marxist, as well as the Congress, rulers have tried their best to send them back home. This is of course a noble cause. But why couldn't they be rehabilitated in Tripura and West Bengal? The vast majority of Tripura is composed of Bengali Hindu refugees from Bangladesh. Why not Chakmas? According to various sources in 1988 more than 125,000 people came to West

Bengal from Bangladesh without visa and settled there. Like Chakmas, did we try to send these Bengalis back? If Thripura was a Chakma state, would this have happened? (Chakmas were finally pushed back in late 1990s after 30 years in hell called 'refugee camp,' but not one other colonizing Hindu refugee or Muslim settler was sent back). As we were able to grab power, we did not want to look back to those whom we left behind. On the other hand, as we were able to grab power in India, our majority-Muslim neighbors in Bangladesh, and before that in Pakistan, didn't want to embrace us. Thus many in Bangladesh consider us as opportunist. Supposedly we did not participate in the local 'causes', although we called that our homeland. In Bangladesh, the first and foremost struggle of Hindus is their struggle for survival.

When I was growing up in Calcutta, I used to hear from friends and relatives that a 'Raja (king) of a that place' fled to India in 1949 and once again became a 'king' in this side of Bengal; or how an East Bengal District Magistrate, Police Chief, Minister, Member of Assembly, or college principal transformed themselves into the same office after moving to Calcutta at different time. During my boyhood, I used to be proud of it. Now I do not have that feeling a bit, especially those who say, "Everything was fine, we just came for no reason." It is, of course, a different issue with those who came 'With only shirt/sari on their back,' or those whose 'last precious possession were taken away at the Benapole Border,' or 'after three days on foot who collapsed on the Agartala (Tripura) border.' I salute them for their struggle to survive. I offer my *Pranam* with deep respect.

It is worth noting that the West Bengali natives, the *Ghotis*, must be one of the most generous people on earth. There is hardly any parallel on earth when an indigenous group welcomed others giving up everything, their land, their jobs and their resources.

Of late, after Bangladeshi independence, many intellectuals and opinion makers are visiting each other's nation, but frequently their reports are either misleading, or at times totally unreal. Often it is the opposite of the reality. We write on the basis of our individual tourist experience, but it seldom reflects on the social-communal reality of the permanent dwellers. In (March though June) 1986 a series of articles were written in weekly *Desh* by a well respected West Bengali politician about visit to his *desh* homeland decades after his departure. Of the three pictures there was a picture of man wearing traditional *dhuti* waist garment. Readers many naturally assume that this is a normal wear as in West Bengal, but most, especially Hindus know how distant this is from the reality. Then he had a picture of a famous old Hindu *Mott* temple. But the *Mott* is still there but a few days before his visit there were attempts to destroy it but there was no mention of that. A few days after that in 1987 a world famous Bangladeshi-origin Hindu Bengali economist was honored at a social science meeting in Bangladesh, when he visited his ancestral home at Wari neighborhood of Dhaka City. But many overseas Bangladeshis objected to inviting the same man to a meeting at his own prestigious university in a foreign country. One Abdul Momen, a Muslim, reader criticized the local group in an overseas paper:

"Objections are raised from many angles, for example, they are foreigners, What do they know about us? Discussions will be held in our language, so how can we bring some outsiders? Recently there have been objections about (that professor.)......there was a proposal for to lecture on 'The Struggle for Bangladeshi Self-Determination and Economic Freedom.' ....He spent his boyhood in Dhaka.......He is also a great speaker in Bengali. But he was rejected as if we've to have someone with Bangladeshi citizenship........Time has come for us to rethink this......" There are but few examples. Recent novels on two

Bengals are perpetuating these ideas. But when we visit each other why don't' we notice these? We need to think about that. And when we notice those, should we not write about that? Inspite of frequent visits by our ministers, journalists, singers, sportsmen, researchers after Bangladeshi independence there hasn't been any noticeable change in the mindset. In the capitalist countries there have always been objections and protests against oppression. As have been with the socialist countries. Lots of protests were lodged by China, by the Party and by peoples against the killing of minority Chinese in Indonesia, and against persecution of the Chinese by the Vietnamese. Similarly socialist Hungary protested against persecution of Hungarian minority in Rumania. And from Albania against Albanians in Yugoslavia. Such examples can be cited from the former Soviet Union, Mongolia, Vietnam and Cambodia.

In the introduction of Dakshina Ranjan Basu's reprinted 1975 book, *"Villages we Left Behind"* it mentions that "the people of the liberated Bangladesh are eagerly waiting for this book." May be. I believe many such documents needed to be written. But did it truly have effects on the minds of Bangladeshis? Are the conditions of the Hindus any better than it was in 1947? I passed by Dhamrai town in Dhaka district several times, but I couldn't stop there, until recently. My friend A. M. Daud, a Muslim, proudly mentioned that his town had one of best *Raths* of the entire Indian Subcontinent for the Hindu chariot festival, the six-storied wooden transporter. In 1971 the Islamic military set the chariot on fire, and killed many Hindus. Now there is only a small chariot, just as a symbol. Reading about Dhamrai he came to know many things with its Hindu past. Still he feels that the, "Hindus have left for no reason."

In our euphoria one thing that is immorally never mentioned is Bangladesh-Pakistan's Enemy Property Act (renamed Vested

Property Act). Through the aid of this racist act Bangladesh Government, its Muslim leaders, middle-class and influential persons have forcibly taken away, without any compensation, hundreds of thousands of acres of farm land, tens of thousands of homes, mansions, ponds farms, shops and business beloging to Hindus. Along with Hindu minority Christians, Buddhists and tribes have suffered, although the act targets only Hindus. Of late some Bihari (Urdu-speaking Indian Muslim migrants from the state of Bihar in eastern India) and once in a while anti-government Muslims are targeted (though the law cannot be used against Muslims). In general the upper and middle class Muslims have benefited from these confiscations, but they have remained silent about that. So have we. Some have compared this mass confiscation property with the land confiscation of Black Africans in South Africa, and that of the confiscation of Jewish properties by Nazi Germany. People are becoming homeless without any compensation, and without any notice. So, we should think once more amidst our nostalgia whether or not we should remain blind in love of our *desh* homeland.

On the other hand, in the first 'Bangladesh Conference' in North America held in 1987 in Washington D.C. Some Bangladeshis became identified as 'pro-India' who had proposed to invite Bengalis from West Bengal. But it was not to be. Though many Americans, Pakistanis, Turks were invited as participants; not a single soul from West Bengal was invited. There were between 8 and 10 individuals with 'Hindu names' present, out of which two were Bangladeshi-Indian. A Hindu sadly commented "a Bangladeshi leader looking at me commented 'how come, so many Hindus are here (in faraway wealthy United States)?' Though the leader didn't mean any insult, but it sounded really harsh. Out of 400-500 people only 8-10 were Hindus i.e. only 2 to 3% which according to Hindu population (then 12%; in 2001 it was down

to less than 10%,) in Bangladesh, it should have been at least 40-
50 persons. As Bangladesh is devoid of her minorities in civil,
military, police, district and national administration, ministries,
embassies or delegates to the U.N (according to a Bangladeshi
sociologist it is 'Bangladeshi Apartheid') that minor presence looks
over-representation to the elites. A similar incidence took place
at the 2nd conference held in New York.

If we avoid the reality then misunderstanding and bitterness
between the two countries and two communities will bound to
rise. And one of the reasons bitterness is being created, is the
character of the middle-class to avoid the unpleasant truth.
Because of the decline of West Bengal and for our failure we
have always used (Central Government at) Delhi as a scapegoat
for real or imaginary reasons. From the pre-independence colonial
days we have been fighting against Delhi. Bangladesh has been
influenced by this as well. Delhi is the scapegoat for them as well,
but the minority Hindus has become entangled with that. Delhi is
far off, so if Delhi is not at hand, we can kill some minorities, drive
them out of thier homes, or torch their Hindu *mandirs*, Christian
churches, and Buddhist *vihars*. And the conspicuous silence of
West Bengal encourages the mayhem. 'Silence is golden.' Above
all we have always held Delhi responsible for the problems of
Bangladeshi Hindu refugees in West Bengal. Bangladesh (and
Pakistan) has done the same. A vast number of Calcutta middle-
class calls Bangladesh's Dhaka-Khulna-Chittagong as their *desh*
home, yet how many times have they held its rulers responsible
for their plight? Is this a new kind of discrimination? Flooding in
Bangladesh is well known. Farakka barrage stands on Ganga
(Ganges) in West Bengal (before Ganga enters Bangladesh). Thus
some Bangladeshis hold India and responsible for their flooding,
that India has been creating excessive rain; that India is cutting
down trees in Nepal, Bhutan and Tibet to harm Bangladesh (in

the down stream); India has been (artificially) melting snow in the Himalayas; they are (secretly) releasing excessive water from (secret) dams. Besides, the water from Farakka barrage is being diverted to the northern Indian states of Rajasthan and Uttar Pradesh, over a thousand miles away upstream. In 1988 a professor in a U.S. publication by Bangladesh Progressive Forum wrote that West Bengal needs Farakka for Calcutta's beautification, and the primary reason was to make fertile the desert-like arid land of Uttar Pradesh, hundreds of miles upstream. And Farakka was responsible for increasing upstream water in the districts or Sylhet, Mymansing, Rangpur and Dinajpur (with which Ganga has no connection). This is one side of the story. On the other side propaganda continues in the hot months, 'North Bengal of Bangladesh' north of the river flow, 'is becoming a desert due to Farakka.' Many in Bangladesh now believe that Farakka is responsible both for floods as well as droughts from Dinajpur (northwest) to Sylhet (northeast), Khulna (southwest) to Chhittagong Hill Tracts (southeast). With this a myth has taken hold. That the leaders of West Bengal have said that West Bengal has no problem with Bangladesh, but like Bangladesh, with Delhi. Many visits by ministers to their homeland and statements at Bangladeshi press conferences they have allegedly said, "West Bengal has no need of Farakka." In the nations of the Subcontinent where 65% are illiterate, and are guided by emotion, there spoken words and myths play very important roles. Many think that the *Bangals* or Bangladeshis in India will look after their interests in India, instead of looking after the well being of India. Similarly, our nature of blaming Delhi for the Bangladeshi Hindu refugee problem in West Bengal, many Bangladeshis believe that the refugees were created by Delhi, and it is Delhi's fault, and no Bangladeshi suffer from any sense of social, political, economic, mental or moral guilt for the 30 million refugees (45 million with off-spring). There are exceptions of course. That's the saving grace. I believe we are directly responsible for this frame of mind. In a Bengal Studies Conference held at Bucknell University in Pennsylvania, someone asked when the issue of 'India's responsibility for all the ills in Bangladesh' was discussed, what has Bangladesh contemplated doing with the tens of millions of Bengladeshi refugees in India? The reply can be found from the comment of former Bangladeshi Foreign Minister, Humayun Rashid Chowdhury, in response to Assam and Tripura citizens' demand for expulsion of Bangladeshis from their states. He said, "There is no Bangladeshi in India." Joining this, what we *bhadraloks*, civilized men, do not say is that 'They are Hindus and Buddhists.' According to them, people have left their home out of their own volition, they are not refugees but colonialists, like the people who have gone to America, and that's why there's no obligation towards them. According to a West Bengal Police report of early 1980s, over 125,000 Bangladeshis had illegally settled in one year in West Bengal while visiting legally through visa. I personally know a number of families who left Barisal, Mahilara and Narayanganj in Bangladesh only between 1982 and 1985. "Under pressure," they said. But I know only a few individuals. They left their ancestral home of tens of generations, silently under the cover of darkness. It may not be an oversimplification to say that Bangla minorities who are coming overseas, although deeply love their home, but are quite bitter and disgusted about the socio-political life.

Bangla political elites have been enjoined in their attitude with a section of her intellectuals and middle-class. West Bengal have joined indirectly. There is no point in blaming one individual president, military general, party leader or a Maulana Islamic preacher. But when needed, we must do so, as those individuals have immense power; which we normally do not do. Decades ago a top lady bureaucrat of Dhaka confided with me, "The situation with our minorities, and outside with the Indians, are like the Jews of Nazi Germany. They are blamed for all the ills of the country. Too much rain or too little. For flood or drought." (In a July 2003 New York City conference, Dr. M. Siddique, a Muslim by birth, of Washington D.C. used that 'Nazi' comparison again). A journalist once reminded me, "Many Bangladeshis say that 'India is swallowing us,' but I think just the reverse is true. The way tens of millions of our people have settled in the East and North-East of India, it seems we've expanded. We have become expansionist just like European settlements in North and South America." Needless to say one should not be anti-Muslim in order to criticize the public policies of the elites and rulers. We must speak with the support of Bengalis and non-Bengalis, Hindus, Muslims, Christians, rightists, leftists, Indians, Bangladeshis, East Bengali, *Bangals* and West Bengali *Ghotis*.

It is difficult to predict what will be the effect on society, economy and politics of this huge population migration. But could any one imagine a short while ago that the old established orders will be challenged in India by the separatist Sikh Khalistani, North Bengal Gorkha, Tripuri of Tripura tribe, and Asom of Assam movements? Or, could someone imagine that the Urdu-speaking Mojahir privileged Indian Muslim migrants will start a movement to protect themselves in Pakistan? Burma and Sri Lanka have witnessed the deprivation of citizenship to the minorities. In South and North America conflict still persists between the 'old' and 'new' residents after 500 years, even when speaking the same language and following the same religion. In socialist and former-socialist countries, new settlements have not solved ethnic problems in places like in Inner-Mongolia (only 14%, Mongols), Tibet (50% Tibetans), Estonia, Latvia, Armenia, Azerbaijan, former Yugoslavia and Romania.

The intellectuals of West Bengal and Bangladesh leaving aside their *bhadralok* meekness, going beyond myth and nostalgia must discuss the matters with the other bureaucrats and intellectuals, if necessary, should confront them. They must protest against persecution. From 1986 through 2003 I wrote several articles about relations between two nations. Many people accused me being either 'pro-Hindu' or 'pro-Muslim.' But I was pleased to see the interest on that issue. An economist and another journalist once told me, "We've a disease-like taboo in discussing our own problems with each other. Either seeing danger we are behaving like an ostrich or in the name of politics we running after a mirage."

Chapter 9
Red Building, Blue Building
(1)

Let's assume that the name of a state capital of a nation is 'Squabble City.' This is my *desh* home. How could a capital have such a name? Well, this is a story, and in story everything's possible. Actually the founders of the city wanted to name it 'Squabble Prevention City.' But some residents say in a hurry someone forgot to add the word 'Prevention.' The mischievous ones say that it was done willfully. Pundits, people with foresight, thought that it will be a place where people will congregate to resolve squabbling to build a peaceful nation.

In that capital I went to the 'Red Building' on that appointed time. *Udoi-babu*, Mr. Udoi, asked to meet him at 1 PM in the afternoon. Mr. Udoi is the left-hand man of *Ranjit-babu*. And Mr. Ranjit is the state's 'Metro Minister.' As city's trams and buses run at a snail's pace, I took a taxi to reach the building 15 minutes before 1 PM. I asked the police guarding the gate, "Which gate should I take? I have to go to that room."

He signaled with his hand, "Take 'Pass' from that place." I noticed that a big sign proclaims of that 'Pass.' When I asked about that pass, a gentleman un-gentlemanly told me, "Come back after 2 PM."

"What? I have to go. I've an appointment at 1 PM."

"Then why didn't you come early? From 1 PM to 2 PM is our Tiffin (lunch) time. With this tremendous pressure of work at this Red Building you people won't even allow us to have our tiffin!"

"I must go. I've come a long way." Then I said to myself that 'just a few years back I had worked here. In this bureaucracy! But, What is this?'

The man angrily said, "Is this the 'Land of the *Moghs*' (land of anarchy)? Do we have to serve for your convenience?"

"For sure! In my *desh* home we say government employees are workers for the public, servant. Because, they are supported by our tax money." This slipped out of my mouth.

"Don't talk that nonsense. We've police and security here." These days even babies are not afraid of police, as we were when we were kids. So, I couldn't understand why he was trying to scare me through that. A few years back when I went to the Red Building with my wife then one of the clerk-gentlemen couldn't figure out how to welcome us. And what is this? In the meantime couple of policemen had arrived there. They were listening to our conversation. Hearing my story again, one of them said to a second, "Hey, let this *shala* (bastard) go." The third police showed me another gate and instructed, "Go to that gate." At that gate, I started from the beginning again. This time it was a modern gate-keeper, and after many phone calls and interrogation I was allowed to go. By that time I was fifteen minutes late.

To Mr. Personal Secretary Udoi-babu I begged pardon for being 15 minutes late. After seeing me, he was so shocked as if a meteorite hit him. "Oh, yes, I asked you to come, but I didn't realize that you would come." In my surprise I must have stayed still for minutes with my mouth wide open. Finally, Mr. Personal Secretary said, "Please have a seat. Once I am done talking to this gentleman, I'd talk to you." As I sat down, Mr. This and Mrs. That kept on coming and going, but I was not getting my invitation. One of the 'peons' (orderly) of one of the *Babus* (ministers and top bureaucrats) counseled me, "You are still sitting here, mister. Go, just push yourself in through the door. I'm working for the

Babus for over 25 years. I know what works here. Can't you see so many people are coming and going? You won't succeed without that." At last, I did that. Mr. Personal Secretary turned me away, "I'll call you right away." I sat once more. One Mr. Kind-hearted peon of the Babus asked, "Is he going to give you a job? Is that why you're here?"

"No."

"An apartment 'flat'?"

"No."

"Land."

"No. But, what are you talking? How would be able to give those?"

"Party?"

"Is he giving a party? When?"

"No, not that kind of a party. Then why have you come here?" I explained them that for a faraway land a book of the 300th anniversary of the City of the Goddess Kali is being published, and I've come to know if Mr. Metro would like to write something in that book. Mr. Kind-hearted remarked, "Haven't you come through the Party?"

"I didn't understand your puzzle."

"Don't you know that if one has to see someone like that man, one must have a written note from the political party? Or, you should have had someone telephone for you. Don't you see that you are sitting here for so long? How are these people going to the minister's room? Didn't you pay someone for this?"

"Why should I give money? A while ago I met Mr. Mayor. Without any hassle he immediately met with me. Do they belong to the same party?"

"That's like winning a lottery. If you are able to get your work done with your efforts, I'm willing to have my name changed from Mr. Kind-hearted to Mr. Wretched."

Mr. Kind-hearted didn't have to change his name to Mr. Wretched. Finally I was to able to see Mr. Lefthand. As he couldn't find my letter, he asked me to make a new application with my intention. I gave him that, immediately, along with my card and the two-page content and description of the proposed book and its writers. He looked at the materials, then said, "No, it won't work. The letter must be typed, and in official pad". As I was leaving, the man-with-unchanged-name asked, "Do you have to come again?" After hearing, he said, "That's nonsense. I've seen so many ministers through these decades. This is the era of corruption, bribery." I objected, "On my last visit I met with minister, Mr. Spell-driver, *Bipod-taron*. After one telephone call I was invited to his house. I really enjoyed it. The Communist minister lives in an affluent neighborhood. He brought tea by himself. With that, *pitha* pancakes and *moa* puffed-rice-ball."

"Oh, Mr. Spell-driver? He is a real learned man, pundit. I believe he lived in your faraway home. He is also from Parbatipur, like you. May be, it is because of that you were able to see him so easily." I vehemently objected to that. But, I still remember that as soon as I entered he asked, "Aren't you from Parbatipur? Your name suggests that. Have you been to Parbatipur? Have you ever eaten her *pitha* and *moa*?"

(2)

A man called me at the residence of Mr. Kamol Abul Fazl, my Muslim friend. Kamol's wife Beena gave me the phone, "Dada, elder brother, your phone." From the other side someone said, "*Aadab*," a Muslim greeting, "Are you Dr. Dastidar?"

"*Aadab. Namaskar*. Greetings. I can't recognize you."

"Ghosh Dastidar?"

"Yes."

"Are you the friend of such-and-such? Are you from there?"

"Yes."

He was relieved. Said, "Namaskar. I am Adityo Bauri." Adityo is a Hindu from the traditionally-oppressed caste. "I'm a bureaucrat of your *desh* home. I'm a classmate of Rwoshan (a Muslim). That Rwoshan, at whose home you stayed a few days back. He and I are both from Parbatipur. However, my family moved from Parbatipur to Sylhet, 200 miles northeast, 150 years ago.........," and so much more. It was decided that I'll meet at his office. At that first encounter Adityo asked me to address him in intimate '*tumi*' for you, instead of more formal '*aapni*.' He works in a golden land. That too is my *desh* home. The name of the capital city is Mahadev-pur, the Land of Lord Shiva (Mahadev). But, now-a days most people affectionately call it Shade or Shade Village. There where the top bureaucrats seat is called Blue Building. And at that Blue Building, I've the appointment.

That morning, before I left I couldn't find Adityo's direction. I called a number. "Sir, could please connect me to Adityo Bauri?"

"Who?"

"Adityo. He may be an assistant secretary."

"Here? Do you know where have you called? This is foreign ministry. No persons with names like Adityo Bauri works here."

"How's that possible? May be you are mistaken..........."

"You don't think it is that country." Then he lowered his voice, and said numbers in Bengali, "Try this number. Six, two, one, ..."

I called that number. A man from the other end responded

unmanly, "Do you think this is the Land of the *Moghs*, Land of Anarchy?" I had heard of this Bengali expression before. "You won't find such names in this department." He put his receiver down. I was trying to match description of my *Mogh* friends, but I wasn't able to match. Finally after many tries I was able to get the number from Rwoshan. I arrived one hour before time, and stood in the shade of a big tree opposite the front gate. At first I was alone. Gradually one by one many others stood next to me. It seemed like most of them were from poor or rural families. Couple of them sought my help in completing their forms. People back home, especially rural folks, are quite simple. In a few minute the way they made me as one of their own, I felt like chanting Lord's name in joy, 'Hari bol, Hari bol,' by raising upwards my two hands. Many of them shared their intimate stories. Some had problems with the brother-in-law, others with their neighbors. Someone told stories of stealing of their ponds. One told stories about the greatness of his *Pir*, Islamic saint. Someone offered me a cigarette. In the midst of this, there was only one woman who was occasionally going across the street, then talking to the blue-uniformed police-gate keepers of the Blue Building, then returning back across the street to this side. She'd a blue Bengali-style *durey* stripped sari, with head covered with sari's *ghomta* hood. The last time she was coming to this side, it felt like she was wiping her tears. The No-Name man standing next to me then anxiously asked me, "Why don't you take a look as to what happened? It doesn't look like a good situation."

"No, no. This is her private affair."

"What is private? She's here. You alone should go," ordered one Mr. Anxious.

"What happened? Are they giving you trouble?" I said. Mrs. Durey Sari didn't respond. Then the other man ordered her to talk to me. Mrs. Durey Sari told me in a whisper in my ear that her name is Biroja Rani Sengupta, a Hindu. She whispered that to my ear. Then she told me that, the neighborhood Muslim thugs have abducted her minor daughter and forced an illegal marriage on her, and she is here to see Minister Mr. Valor if he will be able to bring her daughter back. Before she ended my blood-pressure had shot up already. I told this story of the kidnapping to my friends under the tree, but not her religion. My neighbors were even madder. Some of them rolled up their sleeves. In the end, at the request of the gathered crowd, actually by their order, I had to become a man of pretended importance. I asked the blue guard, why aren't they allowing the lady to see Minister Valor. "The lady must meet the assistant of Minister Valor." With a harsh tone Mr. Blue Pants asked me, "Who are you? Her husband?"

"No." I looked at Mrs. Biroja Sengupta. Then replied, "Relation. You can also call me her husband's friend. I am also waiting for 'Gate Pass' and I met with her accidentally."

"Where do you live? *Desh*?"

"Parbatipur, and at a distant land crossing many oceans and many mountains." Mr. Blue Pants didn't trust me. Still, in suspicion, he talked to some other guards, then gave me the telephone, "Please speak here."

From the other side a deputy secretary talked to me in English. "Are you her relative? How long are you overseas?..........." After completing his interrogation, Mr. Deputy Secretary gave permission to Biroja to enter the building. Right there Mrs. Biroja Rani Sengupta bent on to give me *pranam* thanks by touching my feet. I held her up. That was the last I met my relation.

As soon as I returned back to the other side of the road, ·everyone approached me with their question. Mr. Anxious asked,

"What did you say?"

"I said I am related to Mrs. Biroja Sengupta. And I talked in English."

"How's that possible? I thought she belonged to the other religion. How could you tell them that you belong to the other religion?"

"I am from the other religion. My parents belong to the other religion. And how did you figure out that she's from the other religion?"

"Did they believe you? Our stupid police. Who can trust them?"

I explained them again.

"Really? You are from the other religion?" Their eyes were about to pop out. "Please don't mind, we've said many things," they said.

I asked, "Is that good or bad if one belongs to the other religion?" Our new friends stumbled, as if they are looking at a ghost. "Moreover, you've not said any bad thing about anybody. You said that is true."

A middle-aged man with a long beard asked me from the side, "Have they taken away your property? Is that why you are here? These *shalas* (bastards) won't allow you people to live in this country." He came and embraced me. Then there were so much talk.

The guard at the gate was told about my appointment. I reached Adityo's office exactly on the dot. It seems he has arranged for a nice *aadda* chat session. Between 8 and 10 top bureaucrats were there. The ruler-keeper of the nation. I didn't realize that there could be a bull session in the middle of the day in the office. But this was the time for 'tiffin' lunch. It covered from sex to

Shakespeare; Volanath (Lord Shiva) to violence; from Dhaka to Dhakuria (in Calcutta). Among this Mr. Chadrul, a Muslim, presented me his book, and showed me a chapter, 'Our Duty towards You," and asked "please help our oppressed peoples."

"What's that talk?" A man wearing a tie angrily replied, "We are the rulers of the nation. We're the right and left hands of our oppressing Ministers. The entire nation moves at the direction of . our fingers. And him, Mr. Overseas, will save us?" I barely had any free time to talk with Adityo. In the middle of that excitement Adityo and Asgar, his Muslim colleague, indicated, "Tomorrow we are planning to take you a place, Where? We'll let you know later." They didn't need my permission from me for that plan. This is the nature of hospitality in my *desh* home. There were others who decided to join us.

Early in the morning, as we're leaving, I learned that I am heading to meet Adityo and Asgar's mothers to offer my *pronam*, respect. They are making traditional *pitha* pancakes and *moa* puffed-rice-balls. Our destination : Parbatipur.

Chapter 10

Pogroms and Riots in Bangladesh and West Bengal, 1992-93[1]

(Note: In December of 1992 through January of 1993 I was in West Bengal and Bangladesh, and traveled extensively through the former united Bengal. In Calcutta, I found that, public opinion had polarized,[2] and turning anti-Bangladeshi and anti-Muslim in the aftermath of large scale attack and loss suffered by Hindus (non-Muslims). In Bangladesh a section of Bangladeshi press continues to be anti-Indian and anti-Hindu (minority) and demolition of Babri Mosque in faraway Hindi-speaking Uttar Pradesh State has been agitating them. The Muslim Mughal Emperor Zahiruddin Mohammad Babar, who came from Central Asia's Farghana Valley, now divided into Uzbekistan, Tajikistan and Kyrgyzstan, to conquer India, destroyed many Hindu temples, including a Ram Mandir – temple of Lord Ram in the city of Ayodhya in north-central India, that believers believe to have been built at His birth place though disputed by some, and built a Muslim mosque on top of the demolished temple. Muslim rulers had destroyed thousands of Hindu-Buddhist temples during their rule. The major base of West Bengal and Tripura's Left's support has all along has been the Bangladeshi Hindu refugee – since 1947 partition. Both West Bengal and Tripura states are governed by the

---

1. Based on *South Asia Forum Quarterly*, Vol. 6, No 2: Spring, 1993 and Vol.6, No 4: Fall, 1993 articles.
2. *Daily Bartaman*, Calcutta, December 19, 28, 30 and 31, 1992

*Communist Party of India-Marxist and its left allies,
most of whose leaders have chosen not to live in their
Bangladeshi homeland. With continued attack on
Bangladeshi minorities, these refugees many of whose
families still live in Bangladesh, who constitute about
one-third of West Bengal' population of 70 million
people was turning anti-Muslim, were gradually
speaking out against those atrocities. In my discussion
in West Bengal and in Bangladesh – with Hindus and
Muslims – I found a general sense of concern, and this
article has been written in that context.)*

A Note on Communist West Bengal:

In the aftermath of destruction of Babri Mosque (Muslim
mosuqe of Babar) and the pronouncements that came out or did
not come out of our ruling Bengali elites — the politicians, 'the
intellectuals,' the bureaucrats and even some journalists — I kept
asking myself 'what happened to our *Sonar Bangla*, Golden
Bengal (West Bengal and Bangladesh)?' Have we become a
nation of unconscientiously, shameless people? As I traveled
through the cities of Calcutta and Howrah, from the districts of
Medinipur to Birbhum in West Bengal, from the cities of Dhaka
to Comilla, from the districts of Chittagong to Sylhet in Bangladesh,
and places in between, and witnessing the tragic plight of many
families firsthand, I asked many of our elite friends why are they
censoring facts from rest of us? Can *Shonar Bangla* (or *Shonar
Bharat*, Golden India) be built based of lies and deception? Are
we holding Bangladeshi non-Muslim Buddhist, Christian, Hindu
(including tribal) lives hostage to our petty interest? Or, West
Bengal's minority Muslims and non-Bengalis?

In Calcutta, as I went to a neighborhood one affected Hindu
group asked me if I was related to that 'SOB (Communist)

politician' supposedly his name sounded like mine, whereas another Muslim group whispered me with information asking 'are you that (Muslim) journalist?' Supposedly I looked like that journalist. In another neighborhood a Hindu Marwari family from Hindi-speaking western India, whose home and business were destroyed took me into confidence as my friend confided in perfect Bengali. But alas, no politician, no 'intellectual' had visited them, they complained. Only one Congress leader, Ms. Mamata Banerjee, M.P. now belonging to a splinter nationalist Trinamool (grassroots) Congress Party, had the courage to visit the affected areas whereas the ruling Leftists were driven out by riot affected people.[3] Some relief was coming through, but that was also very communal, very racist, at least in my eye. Muslims were giving relief to Muslims, and Hindus to Hindus. In our Communist-run communalism such is the norm. In a bizarre twist a Communist union leader, Mr. Ram Tewari and his fellow unionists, who had gone to march with Muslims and Hindus to protest against the Muslim Babri Mosque destruction were burned alive and cut to pieces by a Muslim mob. The local (Muslim) councilor was supposed to have incited Muslims against Hindus, where over 10,000 Hindus were homeless. No murderer or arsonist was arrested. Some demanded an investigation of that councilor,[4] but the ruling clique would not allow it. In the Muslim Camp neighborhood in eastern Calcutta I visited there were posters 'we want (CPM — Communist Party of India-Marxist) Police Officer's head' in that Communist-run state but no one questioned that officer, whereas affected Hindus were all polarized, and complained that they are not receiving relief as compared to the Muslim victims.[5] Calcutta newspapers and state propaganda

3. *Daily Anandabazar*, Calcutta, December 15, 1992
4. *Daily Bartaman* December 22, 1992
5. *Daily Anandabazar*, December 14, 1992

machines churned out stories of thousand-year old Bengali Muslim-
Hindu communal amity, not telling us that it was because of our
Bengali-style Hindu-Muslim communalism (I prefer to call it racism
since communalism is a form of racism, albeit religious) it was one
of only two provinces that was partitioned, leaving aside Assam
and Kashmir, and number of people killed and displaced since
1947, especially Bangladeshi Hindus would be over 45 million,
including descendants born outside the homeland, will surpass
most well known cases of 'ethnic cleansing' of the world. Why
this lie? Great speeches were made, poems were written, stories
came out of the finest pens as to how communal 'they' have
become, compared to 'us'- the secular, atheist, Marxists,
socialists, Congressites. Most of these 'secularists' are Hindu
refugees (in India they are called *Bangals*), Bangladeshi-Indian
Bhadraloks (gentlemen) who chose not to live with their Muslim
and oppressed-caste Hindus or could not live in their Muslim-
majority homeland to come to 'Hindu' India. It is a well kept
Bengali secret in India, especially of the politically active Hindu
'secularists,' 'Hinduites' (pro-Hindu) and 'atheists' as to how
they leave their homeland in Bangladesh while simultaneously
denouncing Hindu India. These are the people who write and
speak about 'hidden' communalism of others while making India
more Hindu! Could Sonar Bangla afford to have room for these
types of double standard? Visits to England, France, China, Russia
and the U.S. is preferable than to their homeland. Reasons given
can hardly be printed here. Some of these people are undoubtedly
racist-Communists, anti-Gandhi Congressites (Congress Party
members; Gandhi was the leader of the pro-secular, pro-
independence Congress Party), anti-social socialists, as many of
my friends suggest, while others are now outright anti-Muslim.
While Gandhiji came to Bengal (in 1946-1947) to stop a Hindu
genocide in Muslim-league ruled Bengal (now Bangladesh), these

Congressites were first to desert their Hindu voters (under the separare electoral system) to leave their homeland for India, and of course their Muslim neighbors. This is equally true for our Bengali Hindu Communists and socialists. They have supported riots after riots by either keeping quite, through censoring, or through false propaganda -just as they did during the current 1992-93 riot and pogrom, and now the ghost of these lies are haunting them. I will come to that soon.

Racism of our anti-Muslim Hindu groups or anti-Hindu Muslim groups is quite clear. Both are intolerant of the other, and it is easier to fight, than the covert racism of our so-called secularists. Islamism in Pakistan has succeeded in driving out practically all the non-Muslims – a fifth of the population – from their territory, as well as from Pakistani Azad (Free) Kashmir. Where have all these people vanished? Islamism in Bangladesh has driven her non-Muslims down from about one-third of the population to merely 10% in 2000,[6] in the world's sixth most populous nation. And now many in India want to follow this model.[7] Bangladeshi ruling clique has successfully held the Bangladeshi minority hostage to any imaginary and real happenings in India, especially the bad ones.[8] Through my travel and discussion in India, Pakistan and Bangladesh I have found a group of dedicated intelligentsia who are eager to talk about this. Are we? Openly anti-Hindu Hindu communalists on the other hand had to come up with new definitions of being anti-Muslim while keeping our own form of racism, called casteism, alive. In the infinite toleration preached

---

6. *Bangladesh Statistical Handbook*, 1990, p: 219

7. In India the Hindu nationalists came to power in many states and Federal government in 1996, years after this article was written.

8. In Bangladesh right before a 2001 election an anti-Hindu pogrom began disenfranchising hundreds of thousands of Hindus. A pro-Islam party came to power in coalition with two pro-Taliban parties.

by Hinduism this new gospel has not been easy. Without that toleration and fatalism, casteism could not exist. Thus came the demolition of the Mosque, and that too spearheaded by a 'world Hindu group' whose world is indeed microscopic. They would march to destroy a 400-year old mosque but not to rebuild the 1,200 year-old Ramna Kali Mandir (temple) in Dhaka destroyed by the Army of the Islamic Republic of Pakistan and their Islamist Bengali allies, and then by the newly independent pro-secular Bangladeshi government in 1971-72. They would march to Bangladesh border to stop a 'Long March' but not start a 'relief march' to Indian Muslims and Hindus and for Bangladeshi tribal and non-tribal Hindus, Buddhists, Christians who were affected by the December 1992 pogrom or to rebuild any of the thousand of homes, *mandirs* (temples) and *murtis* (statues of deities), churches, and businesses demolished in 1992. We would worship Goddess Lakshmi and Saraswati but would not touch our sisters Lakshmi and Saraswati who are being gang raped by the thousands just for their namesake. We are becoming pea-brain to pin-head, and humanity is the first casualty. I would have loved to join both the 'Long March' and the 'relief march,' minus, of course, the racism. However, I am afraid, soon Indian Muslims could become hostage to politics to racism in Bangladesh and Pakistan, just as their minorities have been held hostage, killed of cleansed to politics of India with Indian secularists' acquiescence.

What was unique about our Calcutta riot of 1992 is that no one took any responsibility. No one resigned. No one visited the victims: no Prime Minister, no Chief Minister, no Member of (India) Parliament, no Member of (state) Legislative Assembly, no Calcutta Corporation Councilor, no Police Commissioner. My parent's generation wrote it was the worst riot since 1946. I do not know about 1946 riot, but I was a young adult during the 1964 Hazarat Bal Killing in Bangladesh, followed by the Calcutta riot.[9] I thought it was pretty bad then. In Bangladesh it was mentioned that over ten thousand Hindus were killed in cold blood. Washington Post and London Times mentioned that over 1,000 were murdered in the first days of that anti-Hindu pogrom, as did the daily *Anandabazar Patrika* (Calcutta).[10] Dhaka Bengali daily *Ittefaq*[11] while observing strict Pakistani censorship mentioned 'even Muslims are getting killed while trying to save their (Hindu) neighbors.' Two years ago in 1990 after another anti-Hindu pogrom M. Rahman wrote in Dhaka that 1990 riot reminded him of 1964 pogrom when he 'saw Hindu dead bodies all over paddy fields and floating down rivers.' And 1992 riot was many times more severe than 1964 riot, except possibly fewer deaths. In 1964, the Calcutta dailies of *Anandabazar*, *Jugantar*, and *Statesman* all wrote about the plight of minorities there. But not this time though! In 1964 West Bengal Chief Minister Prafulla Chandra Sen admitted that 25 Muslims and another 25 Hindus were killed in Calcutta, India rioting.[12] What happened to West Bengal's Administration this time? In 1964 some in West Bengal's opposition Communist parties wanted resignation of some of the ruling Congress ministers.[13] Some of those parties in opposition are now rulers of Bengal. Why nobody admitted anything? Why nobody resigned? Why nobody asked for any resignation? Where is our democratic value? At the height of rioting then Congress Chief Minister,[14] and Governor Mrs. Padmaja Naidu visited riot

---

9. Over 1.1 million refugees registered with the Gobernment of India. Dandakanya Forests in central India were opened for them; others went to the Andaman Islands.

10. *Daily Anandabazar*, February 8,1964

11. *Anandabazar*, January 15,1964

12. *Anandabazar*, January 20,1964

13. *Anandabazar*, February 15,1964

14. *Anandabazar*, January 15,2004

affected areas.[15] What happened to our Communist Chief Minister Jyoti Basu or to our Governor in 1992? Even one Bangladeshi-Indian Chief Minister, Mr. Prafulla Chandra Ghosh,[16] who had deserted his homeland earlier in 1947, had courage to attempt to visit the oppressed in Bangladesh, then called East Pakistan in 1964. And in 1992? We have two Bangladeshi-Indian Chief Ministers now in West Bengal and Tripura. In 1964 many in the Left, Right and Center felt enough pain to raise the issue of 'population exchange[17] between Hindu Pakistanis (Bangladeshi of today) and Muslim Indians. Where is our pain in 1992, either for our West Bengali minorities or majorities, or for our Bangladeshi minorities? Saddest part of my *Sonar Bangla* experience has been how so many now feel that the only solution to minority problems in Bangladesh (and now in India) is population exchange, as had happened with Pakistan. If anti-Muslim racism is rising in West Bengal, it is not enough to blame Hindu or Muslim communalism, a large part of the 'blame' lies with the actions, not the deeds, of our covert racism of the Communists and of the Left and secularists.

This time around in Calcutta, in typical Hindu Bengali style we all looked for scapegoats for our deeds : the Promoters, Emperors and Bears — names of state-supported gangs, Reactionaries. These are new code words for new forms of communalism. Then there were Urdu-speaking-Bangladeshis[18] who were settled by the politicians 'without proper secular education,' wrote one

---

15. *Anandabazar*, January 18, 2004
16. *Anandabazar*, February 8, 2004
17. *Anandabazar*, February 6, 2004
18. For Urdu Speaking Bangladeshis in Calcutta, see Dr. Amalendu De, *Bangladesher Janabinyas O Sankhalaghu Samassya* (Population Growth in Bangladesh & Her Minority Problem), Ratna, Calcutta, 1992

paper[19] and who were supposedly active against Hindus in certain neighborhoods. Why could the politicians not arrest those Promoters, and Hindu and Muslim gang leaders named Emperor or Bear? Why did they settle some of the Urdu-speaking Bangladeshis when many of their leaders had openly mass murdered Hindu Bengalis and secular Muslims during Bangladeshi Liberation War, and when they wanted to go to Pakistan? Now the Right is asking this question : Why the leaders are rewarding murder of our relatives? What kind of secularism is that? Would such acts have gone unpunished in Communist Soviet Union or China? Or in democratic Europe or in the U.S.? A hopeful sign amidst one of the most serious tragedies of the world has been that a dedicated group of true secularists - without any specific political affiliation, are coming forward to look beyond their narrow nationalism and work together across the partitioned border to come to a humane solution.

A Note on Islamized Bangladesh :

I was in Bangladesh and India during and after the disturbances that followed the Babri Mosque destruction. However, what happened in Bangladesh with their non-Muslim minorities is certainly extremely serious, as reported by the Bengali press in Bangladesh and West Bengal,[20] and what I witnessed in West Bengal, although hardly anybody took note of that fact outside

---

19. *Statesman*, Calcutta, December 16, 1992
20.   Shafi Ahmed & Purobi Basu (Eds.), *Akhono Gelona Andhar* (Darkness hasn't gone yet), Sahitya Samabai, Dhaka, 1993: Mafidul Haque & Arun Sen (Eds.), *Dhwangshstupey Alo* (Light in the ashes), Dhaka Sahitya Prakash and Calcutta Protikshan publication, 1993. Also see special issues of *Frontline*, daily *Bartaman*, weekly *India Today*, December 1992: Shariyr Kabir, *Bangladeshi Sampradaiykatar Chalchitra* (Portrait of Communalism in Bangladesh), Jatio Shahitya Prakashani, Dhaka, 1993

the Bengali press. However, in West Bengal where Bangladeshi refugees since 1947 partition constitute at least one-third of the state's 70 million people, and two-thirds of Tripura state's population, mood is increasingly turning anti-Bangladeshi. I am afraid that this twist of psyche might turn anti-Muslim unless situation in the region is discussed together with open mind. West Bengal Communists postponed village *panchayat* (local government) election in West Bengal twice, while Congress rulers postponed Tripura election once. Both the Chief Ministers Jyoti Basu (West Bengal) and Samir Barman (Tripura) in 1992 were from Bangladesh, so are many of the Indian elites including many of the Federal ministers and ambassadors.

After initial Government and Islamic intimidation several Bangladeshi papers printed some of the atrocities committed on their Hindu minorities. Prime Minister Mrs. Khaleda Zia on the other hand not only completely denied everything about the anti-minority riots but also went further and thanked her supporters for 'maintaining communal peace,'[21] as did the anti-minority Islamists. The situation was so desperate that all the eleven Hindu, Buddhist, Christian Members of (Bangladesh) Parliament, including tribal, (out of a total of 330 Members of Parliament) - government supporters as well as those in opposition, wrote on January 4, 1993 in a statement to the nation and the world :

'Today we meet with you with a devastating and broken heart. We are angry, stunned... The way in which religious minorities in our country are subjected to repeated oppression-repression in the pretext of happenings in another country, there is no parallel in the history of the world...

'...According to reports received so far thousands upon thousands of temples, churches, places of worship, businesses,

21.   Shafi Ahmed in daily *Banglabazar Patrika*, December 25, 1992

and homes have been looted, destroyed, or set on fire. Villages after villages have been destroyed. 43 (of the 64) districts have witnessed destruction (pogrom) including Dhaka, Chittagong, Bhola, Manikganj, Coxbazar, Sylhet, Sunamganj, Pabna, Dinajpur, Khulna, Barisal, Pirojpur, Narayanganj, Kushtia, Maulavi Bazar, Faridpur, Gopalganj, Comilla, Feni, Noakhali. It is even continuing to this day.

'Over 200,000 individuals have lost everything and are spending helpless nights in (only in eight districts of) Bhola, Manikganj, Chittagong's Sitakunda and Mirersarai, Gopalganj, Noakhali, Sylhet, Sunamganj, Coxbazar, and Kutubdia alone. Government has not taken any step to protect them. No relief has been provided to them. Not only Government is not sending any relief, but also they are not giving permission to provide any relief by other organizations...

'...Thousands of families are spending winter nights under open sky. They have no clothing, no food, and no place to hide. Thousands of our mothers and sisters have lost their voice after being violated. ...They are being forced to give up their property. Attempts are being made to forcefully convert these hapless people. Criminals are freely moving around. Nothing is being done against them; (police) is not taking their complaints.

'We are really at pains to mention that our Prime Minister (Mrs. Khaleda Zia of the pro-Islam Bangladesh Nationalist Party-Ed) has not shown slightest remorse, and she has not visited any affected area. She has even completely denied the reality........

'According to the data that we have gathered so far 28,000 homes have been destroyed, including 9,500 which have been

completely destroyed and 2,700 businesses have been destroyed, and 3,600 temples and places of worship, ... have been damaged or completely destroyed. In this pogrom 12 individuals have been killed, and another 2,000 individuals have been wounded. Over 2,600 women have been oppressed.[22] *In this attack Buddhist and Hindu monks have not been spared either. Initial estimate of loss is over 2 billion takas...'*

In Bangladesh there has never been any incident when the minority attacked or showed any disrespect to any majority religious institutions, as it frequently happens in other countries like Bosnia, Croatia, India, Iraq, Northern Ireland, Palestine-Israel, South Africa, Sind (Pakistani province), etc., thus it is less of a 'riot' than a 'pogrom.' Even before 1992 attack several writers in Bangladesh have written about this in newspapers and journals.

'In the context of present-day reality' the parliamentarians demanded immediate relief for the riot victims; reconstruction of homes, businesses, properties and temples; arrest and conviction of murders, rapists and other criminals, banning of communal politics; prosecution of people for administrative and police inaction; and permanent solution of minority problems.[23] In my travel through the villages and towns of Bangladesh, from her capital city of Dhaka to the remotest corners, I found villages after villages completely razed, people homeless, temples completely gutted, crops burned, and families forced to sleep

---

22. Rape is a word never used in Bengali families. For many it is worse than death.
23. Statement circulated by Bangladeshi non-Mulsim minority MPs at a press conference at the Bangladesh Press Club in the capital city of Dhaka on January 4, 1993. Also see Binod Dasgupta in daily *Banglabazar Patrika*, Dhaka, December 29, 1992, and Ershadul Haq, *India Abroad*, New York, February 19, 1993.

under winter open sky. This is several weeks after the pogrom since the government completely denied the facts, her Administration discouraged and sometimes opposed distribution of relief, even when geven by minorities themselves or by secular groups.[24] The situation was so critical that on April 10, 1993, at the opening of South Asian nations' (SAARC) gathering in Dhaka the Hindu minorities, along with their Chiristian, Buddhist and secular Muslim cousins, decided to go on fast as a protest of government's inaction. Apart from local groups it is the Bangladesh Ramakrishna Mission and other Hindu-Buddhists ashrams that had been providing relief, in spite of their limited resources. Scores of Hindu Ramakrishna Missions and minority student dormitories were set on fire, and several *smasans* (cremation areas) have been destroyed. Islamists have been attacking, destroying, and confiscating *smasans* for quite some time, and in many areas it is becoming difficult to provide last rites to Hindus and Buddhists. Several of these destroyed *smasans* I visited myself. Christian cemeteries were being desecrated as well. Gandhian Abhoy Ashram of Nonviolence in Comilla City was also gutted. Hundreds, perhaps thousands, of Hindu girls were raped and tens of thousands of Hindus were kept 'naked' in the cold winter, especially in the District of Bhola Island, as mentioned by the MPs. This was reported not only by newspapers but also by the local Member of Parliament Mr. Tofail Ahmed, a Muslim.[25] For months he has also been demanding that government provide some relief, without much success. In Bangladesh hardly any minority had been helped in repairing their homes, businesses and places of worship. No rapist or murderer was arrested, although the

---

24. Shafi Ahmed in *Banglabazar Patrika* daily, December 25, 1992
25. See Tofail Ahmed, M.P. from Bhola, reported in daily *Bhorer Kagoj*, Dhaka and weekly *Probashi*, New York, January 29, 1993, and Kuldip Nayar, *India Abroad*, February 19, 1993

administration enacted such a law in 1992 to prosecute criminals. Minorities were being asked to leave the country and go to India. Incidentally, minorities also blamed the established opposition, leaving aside the leftist parties, for attack on them. Communist Party neadquarters in Dhaka and the Indian Library and India Airlines' offices were set on fire. As there are true secularists in Bangadesh, howsoever microscopic they might have become. Similar non-party individuals from Calcutta came forward to write an open letter 'To the Intellectuals and Creative People of Bangladesh from Their Indian Brothers and Sisters,' realizing the gravity of the Bangladeshi minority situation is having on the Communist-run West Bengal. Parts of the appeal read:

'Today all of you are engaged in a grim battle to save [the] legacy of the Bangladesh Revolution from the renewed and combined onslaught of the fundamentalist forces......The negative communal and fundamentalist forces were sufficiently marginalized (in India). But the winds of fundamentalism that had swept through the neighboring countries corroding those values that sustain and strengthen progressive societies have given them a shot in the arm. The large scale and ceaseless migration of people in the face denial of human and civil rights has not only caused serious economic strains and social and political conflicts on narrow communal lines but has become a major factor for the growth of fundamentalism in our country.....'

'.....But let us forget that neither secularism nor democracy can survive unless plurality is welcomed and encouraged (by allowing minorities to live) .... (In the aftermath of Ayodhya mosque demolition) the Government and most political parties and the people (of India) have combined to resist this onslaught of obscurantism. Should this message

fail to evoke a warm fraternal response from our neighbors,
we shudder to think of the consequences. Therefore, with all
the strength and goodwill at our command, we appeal to you
all on this auspicious day to stand by the minorities of your
country and help us in our battle. We, in India are sworn to
stand by the minorities of this country and help you in your
battle...'

The appeal was signed by thirteen eminent Hindu and Muslim
scholars, including five ex-Vice Chancellors (university presidents).
Many of the Bangladeshi intelligentsia under the banner of
Sammilito Sanskritik Jote (United Cultural Front) appealed to
Bangladeshis in December 1992 to fight against the Bangladeshi
anti-Hindu pogrom. However, attack against the minorities
continued unabated from 7th through 20th December 1992, and
continued at a smaller scale in 1993 throughout the length and
breadth of the world's sixth most populous nation! The pogram
covered 43 of the 64 districts of that country while its police,
army, paramilitary forces, and the administration looked on. In
the other 21 riot-free districts, except for the three tribal districts
in the Chittagong Hills, non-Muslims have practically been wiped
out since the 1947 partition of Bengal.

Even several weeks after the plunder and attack I did not find
any village or neighborhood that was receiving relief or that was
being rebuilt. No temple, ashram, dormitory, business, home was
being rebuilt. From Calcutta's Communist Party *Ganasakti* and
'reactionary' *Anandabazar* daily to 'capitalist' *New York Times*
to the Islamic newspapers in Bangladesh all have joined together
in hiding the facts. I am not sure if censorship helps this situation
at all, since people often overstate the reality, sometimes
understate. People in turn loose faith with the intelligentsia and in
the media as is happening with the secular intelligentsia in Calcutta.

As Bengali-Indian public opinion polarized the Communist Party of India-Marxist *Ganasakti* and India's largest circulation daily *Anandabazar* printed few skimpy stories about Bangladesh. In the days of mobile telephone, fax, camcorders, and live TV it is difficult to hide the truth. A group of leading Calcutta Muslims, including the former Calcutta High Court Chief Justice, also sent an appeal to all Bengalis to secularize them.

Large scale attack on minorities continued several days after that Indian letter and the Bangladeshi appeal, and with no relief, hundreds of thousands of minorities were barely surviving under the winter open sky. Only hope for survival for many of the 25 million-plus minorities there was to be refugee and go to India. Bangladeshi minorities have come down from a third of the population in 1947 to about one-tenth in 1990. If rest of the Hindu, Buddhist, Christian, tribal Bangladeshis go to India, as has happened in Pakistan, would that be good for South Asia or for *Sonar Bangla*, the Golden Bengal?

Chapter 11
Sri Kanta

Aunirban Anthony Albert D. David thought he was hallucinating as he got up from his bed. Was it a nightmare or was it real? In the middle of the night he received a telephone call from his little sister Anjana, '*Dada*', older brother, '*Didi*, (older sister) is missing. Someone kidnapped her, and told *Baba* (father) that she will be married to a Muslim after a *tabligi* Islamic conversion ceremony. They also warned Baba, if he goes to the police either she will be beheaded or we will be driven away from our home to India.' She pleaded, 'Dada, do something. Please do something.' Then the call stopped abruptly. Either Anjana terminated the call fearing strangers who may hear her and cause her harm, or the manager at the private telephone call office invoked his power over the infidel in the now-fervent Islamic land. Or, may be an 'invisible hand,' as people in the village say, terminated the call. Aunirban knew that there is a long tradition of a large section of majority Muslims to act as 'guardians' of the state and censor minorities or 'make them behave,' but that generally applied to Hindu minorities, not Christian. Still, Aunirban refused to give up and continued saying, 'Hello, hello' for a long time at the dead receiver as if Anjana's voice will somehow appear. Aunirbans did not have telephone at their village home. Not knowing what to do at that time of the night, he tried their Hindu grocer, Nirmalendu Dolui who rents his cell phone to the public several times, but Aunirban couldn't reach his Doluikaka, Uncle Dolui. Dolui rose from the poor oppressed-caste Hindu peasant background to be a marginally-improved grocer, neglected by some of the privileged caste — Hindu and Muslim — elites, and known in the West as untouchable though there was no such term in colloquial Bengali, neither did Hindus behave differently toward people of Dolui's status. His cell phone was the link to the outside world for the David family, and for many other area residents of that remote part of the world. Aunirban repeatedly heard either a peeping busy signal or a soft urbane female recorded voice in Bengali, 'Line is open, please try again.' But, no luck. He then tried his *Jetha* uncle at Dhaka, but his *Jethima* aunt who was at home at the middle of the day hadn't heard the news yet. *Jethima*, father's older brother's wife, said, 'I will ask your *Jetha* Uncle,' her husband, 'to call Chittagong' Aunirban's home district 'immediately.' He then called his school headmaster Lakshmi Narayan Debnath, a Hindu, in the city who immediately left for David home for a two-hour journey, including a half-an-hour hike through the paddy fields. Aunirbans lived in Kaliganj village, barely 18 miles but half-a-day's journey from Chittagong City in the southeast of the country. Chittagong itself is 150 miles from the capital city of Dhaka, but is half-a-day journey following the sleek, modern national highway. Before the highway was built in the 1970s it used to take a day to reach Chittagong, and days by boat. The kidnapped sister Theresa was younger to him, third of six children, and her marriage had already been arranged with a Christian groom from Pabna district, next month, whom Theresa following tradition hadn't met yet, but they were planned to meet soon. Aunirban's parents Surendra Nath and Indrani Das lived in their ancestral village for three generations. It was Surendra Nath's grandfather, Shyama Prasad, a learned man, who took to Christianity and moved away from their neighboring Jhalokathi village. He was an anti-British pro-independence Indian nationalist, and continued to celebrate many of the traditional Hindu festivities that were locally known as Bengali festivities. After the 1947 India and Bengal partition, a part of their extended family moved to India, including his younger brother Jatindra Nath's and older sister

Korunamoyee's families. But seeing the Islamic atrocities against Hindus, and how his Hindu neighbors were forced to leave their homes of hundreds, perhaps thousands of years, and how many of their girls and wives were abducted and forced to convert to Islam, the nationalist Surendra Nath started distancing himself from Hindus for fear that his Indian nationalist credentials and Bengali name may be mistaken for being Hindu. To be fair, most Muslims thought them to be Hindu. Surendra Nath Das transformed himself, after much agony, self-search and discussion with the church pastor, to S. N. D. David, and named his children born after that transformation — Anthony, Margaret, Theresa, Jonathan, Joshua and Annette — different from Hindus and Buddhists who kept Bengali names while Muslims took Arabic, Persian, Turkic or Afghan names. He couldn't give up Das altogether; instead he transformed his family name as 'D. David.' Local Bengalis called Das family's new name as 'English' name, while the family called it Christian. A large number of Muslims also took Bengali nicknames, which became all-but-official name. But, Surendra Nath wouldn't have any Bengali nicknames either, until some of his children grew to be teenagers when without telling their parents took Bengali names. Anthony called himself *Aunirban*, not yet achieved *nirban* or nirvana. Annette took *Anjana*, the eye shadow, and Joshua asked his school home room teacher to call him *Jayanta*, son of Lord Indra. One may call this to be effects of the rising tide of Bengali nationalism beginning in the 1950s, away from the anti-Hindu Islamic separatism of the Indian Muslims of 1920s, 1930s and 1940s which gave birth to Islamic Pakistan in 1947. Anjana has already caused headache for the family, and an outrage at the Christian community, by announcing that she will have a 'love marriage,' breaking family tradition of arranged marriage, with a Hindu, Chanchal Sharma, two year senior in college from an educated yet poor family of privileged Brahmin caste, from the neighboring Palong village. Aunirban's family belonged to the privileged *kayastha* 'warrior' Hindu caste, that was supposed to have been gone with conversion, but the family looked for similar match among Christian families for their children's marriage. One could be sure that there was consternation in that Hindu family as well, but Anjana brought 'shame' to her family when she mentioned that her would-be mother-in-law 'is really nice to her.' Her family's friends and well wishers — Christian, Muslim, Buddhist and Hindu — said, 'It is a shame for the girl to meet the in-laws before her parents have met them. But, then this is *Kali-joog*' modern Kali Era of Hindu scripture polluted by vices.

Although Aunirban had learned from his family the rising tide of anti-Christian violence in the recent past, but living in distant Montreal he wasn't fully convinced of that. He thought either these stories were anti-Muslim or anti-Bangladeshi propaganda that many politicians argued were the deeds of Hindus or of Hindu India's secret service. Or, Aunirban thought that this was just a nightmare that he did not want to believe in and wished that this trend will blow away soon. This anti-Christian phenomenon started in the 1990s after the First Gulf War. Till then the small Christian community was thought to be somehow associated with America and Europe, and as such there was some fear that rich Christian countries somehow could object to killing of Christians, not Hindus. And their aid may be cut off from the aid-dependent nation. Buddhists were also spared for similar reasons for fear of Japan, Thailand and Taiwan's wealth and influence. But not Hindus. During the 1971 Bangladesh Liberation War when the anti-Hindu anti-secularist genocide was committed, both Christian and Buddhist minorities were unharmed. Many Hindus were saved by wearing Christian crosses, sometimes with encouragement of Christian preachers. A Buddhist king, Raja Tridib Roy, even served in the Hindu-killing Islamic Pakistan's Administration and subsequently served as Pakistan's ambassador in many lands for many decades. A leading Buddhist monk, Sri Bishuddhananda Mahathero, closely collaborated with the Army of Islamic Pakistan. Hindu-killers knew Hindus had nowhere to turn to for support, except the local marginalized Hindus or secular Muslims. Many of the fleeing Hindu refugees rose to leadership positions in the Indian Federal Government, as well in the Communist-ruled states of West Bengal and Tripura, bastion of the so-called progressive, leftist and Communist politics of India. But the killers also knew that Indian Hindus, especially Bengali Hindus, do not protest Hindu killing, lest they are called 'anti-Muslim' or 'communal' in India. And for many devout Hindus their fate were already decided, as told in the scripture, or were too self-occupied and fatalist to protest violence against 'someone else' or against themselves. Indian Hindu Bengali progressives, of various shades, vast majority from Muslim-majority Bangladesh, frequently call statewide general strike *'bandhs,'* to protest killing of Muslims in Bosnia, Chechnya, Gujarat, Baghdad, and Kandahar that many of them couldn't even point in a map. Aunirban had learned from his Indian uncle Jatindra Nath that Indian Hindus, especially Bengali Hindus, do not protest when their partitioned families are killed or raped, or brothers and sisters lost forever or when thousands of homes, temples, libraries, and cremation areas are razed to the ground! As Aunirban tried to come to grips of the situation his hallucination gradually turned into anger, and finally to fear as he remembered speeches at a recent meeting that he refused to attend to protest the beheading of Nishith Tripura, a tribal nondescript Hindu man, killing of Hindu SriKanta Rakshit in 2003 when his family refused to leave their beloved Bangladesh for India in spite of many threats, for the Hindu Sil family whose eleven members of were burned to death for being Hindu in November 2003, for blowing the brains

off of Principal Gopal Chandra Muhuri, a Hindu, in November
16, 2001, Buddhist monk Gyan Jyoti Mahasthabir in April 21,
2002, Hindu priestess Mrs. Rani Bala Bhowmik, among a long
list of non-Muslims injured, torched, robbed, raped, murdered,
all in just one corner of the nation. Aunirban's head was already
spinning, as if he was high on ganja (hashish). It reminded him of
Hindu devotees on Shiv Ratri, the night of Lord Shiva, when they
would stay up all night singing, chanting, dancing and praying in
the name of the Lord while consuming ganja and bhang (opium)
to have a feeling of being with the Lord. Lord Shiva is the most
popular of the Holy Trinity : Brahma, Bishnu (Vishnu) and
Maheswar (Shiva) — representing the cycles of birth, life and
death respectively. Shiva is the god of termination to whom all life
must end up for new life to begin. Besides, Shiva is very easy to
please. Aunirban saw this at his village temple, and devotees,
mostly older male, said that such drugs made their head spin,
allowing them to have a feeling of closeness to God. Killing of
Hindus was nothing new; it has been going on from the day of
1947 partition, Aunirban said to himself. Aunirban learned to ignore
these killings like anybody else whether at home in Bangladesh or
like the elites and politicos of India or like the media and rights
activists of America, Europe and rest of the enlightened world.
But, now the horror was closing in on him. He sat down on his
paper-filled dining table looking for newspaper articles on
SriKanta that his Hindu neighbor Gouranga gave him. Thinking
about his sister and re-reading stories about SriKanta, Aunirban
kept saying to himself, a famous early 20th century verse of poet
Tagore :

> Seventy million children, dear Mother charm
> You've made us Bengali, but not human.

Aunirban read the articles, the letters, the paper clippings related to SriKanta — the man with pleasant physique, *i.e.*, Lord Krishna — that were circulated at the meeting over and over again, pacing back and froth from his dinning table to the bedroom window in his cluttered small apartment. Looking at the trees at the landscaped courtyard of the apartment complex Aunirban tried to feel the smell of *jui* (jasmine), *madhabi-lata, nishi-padma* (night queen) and *hashna-hena* flowers someone talked about at SriKanta's home in Chittagong. It was much like his home in Kaliganj that he was trying to imagine.

The Plot :

A family friend of SriKanta told the protest meeting that SriKanta's parents wanted to name their boy after Lord Krishna or Sri Krishna, Kanta being one of the 108 names of the Lord. It is a common custom among Indians to add the honorific Sri, meaning beauty for both male and female names. It also means 'Mr.' or 'Ms.' as in Sri (or Shri) Joe Someone or Sri Jane Lady, but now it is more common to use Sri for men than women, except for goddesses and female saints, as in the nation of Sri Lanka, Sri (Lord) Ram, Sri (Goddess) Durga, Sri (Goddess) Kali, Sri (saint) Mira Bai, Sri (monk-revolutionary) Aurobindo, Sri (guru) Chinmoy, Sri (saint) Chaitanya, and Jane would be written as Srimati Jane Lady. For Lord Krishna, one of the Hindu gods, Sri matches naturally than many other Bengali names. The family friend told the crowd that there was another reason for using Sri in the newborn's name. With the rising Islamization of Bangladesh the ruling elites have taken it upon themselves to erase the Hindu heritage of their ancestors for a new cultural reconstruction. Thus bureaucrats and zealots started using North Indian Muslim word *Janab* for Sri and Begum or Mrs. for Bengali Srimati. Gouranga informed the group that as SriKanta's older brother would write Sri as a prefix before his first name Kumar, as has been the custom for generations including Muslims, some Muslim school teachers would strike it down by writing *Janab* trying to 'Islamize' the nation although his school's students and teaching staff were overwhelmingly Hindu in the majority-Muslim nation. The final high school certificate came with the word *Janab* Kumar and not Sri Kumar. For the younger son the proud parents decided not to depend on the prefix but to incorporate in SriKanta as a compound word. SriKanta's parents had to wait sixteen years till high school certificate to arrive to find how wrong they were when they found out that the name was shrunk to only Kanta from SriKanta, and the certificate read '...*Janab* Kanta.' The prestige of brilliant SriKanta who topped the national exam of hundreds of thousands students couldn't preserve the long tradition. But the family stuck to SriKanta anyway, regardless of the bureaucratic Islamization. It is just not in Bangladesh but even in New York City as late as October 30, 2004 anti-secular pro-Islam Bangladeshis were insulting the pro-tolerant former Bangladeshi Prime Minister Sheikh Hashina Wazed with 'Srimati Hashina Go back to India' banners[1] implying Mrs. Hashina was Hindu for being pro-tolerant thus she must go to India yet the Muslim demonstrators' grandmothers must have addressed themselves as such only decades ago. This trend is similar to the communalization of dress with men giving up their traditional *dhuti* (dhoti) bottom covering, and married women giving up traditional *ghomta* hood-like sari covering over head, for Saudi Muslim head covering and *galabiya* ankle-length Saudi long dress for sari. The tradition still continues across the border among Muslims in non-Muslim India, but change is coming there too. Still when foreign visitors were invited to meet with West Bengal's Communist Law Minister Abdul Razzak Molla, a Muslim, at his Calcutta office, he was wearing the traditional

---

1. *Desh Bangla*, New York City Bengali weekly, October 31, 2004; 44
2. *South Asia Forum Quarterly*, Washington D.C., Fall 1989; 1

Bengali *dhuti*.[2] When asked about the trend in Islamized Bangladesh, he reminded the visitors that his ancestors were wearing *dhuti* for ages, long before the arrival of Islam in Bengal.

There were many stories about SriKanta in the newspapers, with gory details. Mr. Naba, a recent immigrant, volunteered to read one of the articles. Naba however, refused to disclose his full name even in distant Canada for fear of persecution of his family back home. Thus a identity-less nameless Nava read from the brief report at the *The Daily Starr* of Dhaka. April 24, 2003 dateline reported:

Engineer murdered: Two arrested in Chittagong

Detectives yesterday arrested two persons in connection with the brutal

Killing of Computer engineer Srikanta Rakshit from the City's Patenga Area.

Police also traced the spot where the engineer was murdered.

The arrestees..... were believed to be hired by the prime accused in the case, Azimuddin Mahmud, to kill Srikanta, youngest son of senior lawyer Mridul Rakshit, police said.

Police quoted the statements of the two as saying armed criminals picked up Srikanta from in front of Primary Training Institute (PTI) building in the City's Ice Factory road under Double Mooring thana (police station) at around 8:00 pm on last Saturday. They took him to a 4-storied building in the area and slaughtered him.

The killers then took the beheaded body of Srikanta to Tandrabil in Shikarpur union under Hathazari police station by a car and came back to the city, leaving the body there, police said.....

Incidentally beheading of a son, sending body parts to the Hindu mother as warning for her devotion to the land would not be covered at all in the Bangladeshi-Hindu dominated 'progressive' or 'reactionary' press of Calcutta, India or by international correspondents from New York, Washington D.C. or Montreal.

Nicholas (Natu) Costa, a Bengali classmate of SriKanta, with tears in his eyes described how they all were treated with *rasagolla*, Bengali cheese ball sweet dipped in syrup, by SriKanta's parents when 'the result was out. We rejoiced so much that they had to bring in more *rasogolla*. Celebration continued for days!' Natu added, 'He was so bright that he even received a scholarship from Bill Gates. It became national news.' Then he reminisced some of his old childhood memories. He reminded that there were reports in local newspapers that a severed body part was sent to the mother in order to give Hindus and other non-Muslims a lesson as to what could happen to them if they don't give their properties to Muslims and flee Bangladesh for India. 'Already we are down from a third of the population to mere 10% in fifty years, and the killers want rest of us to go to India,' said Costa.

"As Uncle Mrudul fled the city, whenever I called them, Aunt *Mashima*" Srikanta's mother, Natu told, "cried on the phone, saying, 'My son was so innocent and so good, why did *Bhagaban*, God, gave us this punishment?' What can you say to a mother of a murdered innocent child?"

Tarit Hazari, a Hindu rose to read an article from a Bengali paper:

Occupiers of our Property have Killed Srikanta: Going to open a College of Law,

Won't give Property Away

.....Five years ago one influential (Muslim) group illegally took away their hundreds of acres of farm land and their residential property of hundreds of years. They took over the home they were living in. Then the father of the household attorney (advocate) Mridul Kanti Rakshit fled home along with his engineer son and college-going daughter. ...In order to drive them out of the country (for India) they kidnapped the son and brutally killed him...The youngest son Srikanta and his mother stayed at home to protect their property .... the killers after killing kept his head (with them).

Advocate Rakshit told that they (extended family) won (for many generations) two building at Hazari Lane, land worth of millions of takas, in the countryside of Rauzan in the Noapara village they own hundreds of acres of farm land, ponds, and open land. From 1998 a (Muslim) group, led by Azim Uddin Mahmud, started taking over their land and then properties in the city, including the home they were residing in. Another (Muslim) group started taking over their farm land in Chakoria area....The home at Hazari Lane was taken over on 27 December 1998...

Mr. Rakshit did not get any result by approaching the topmost reaches of the (pro-secular) government of the time....[3]

Tarit asked the group, 'How would Canadians and Americans feel if we immigrants just walked into their homes of hundreds of years, and they had to move unconditionally to make room for us without any compensation?' Tragically the meeting could not get blessing from a single 'secular' South Asian, progressive Indian or tolerant Muslim groups. They did not want to be 'tarnished'

3. *New Probashi*, New York City Bengali weekly, April 27, 2003; 36

by raising the killing of Hindus. Exceptions were the known Muslim
personalities of A.B.M. Osman Ali, Dr. Bahar Nuruddin, vendor
Haidar Howladar, housewife-activist Mrs. Suraya Jahan Shurovi,
taxi driver Nuruzzaman and Professor Rafikul Dastagir who were
known both as *kafir*, a non-believer, and *murtad*, anti-Muslim,
to Islam-lovers. Sadly no learned Hindu preacher could be found
to read from the Holy Gita in the memorial-cum-protest gathering.
Keralite-Indian priest Father Kuriakose from South India and
Canadian-Lutheran pastor Reverend Albert quoted from the
scriptures, as did Bengali Buddhist monk Venerable Bodhipal.
Realizing what was happening, a middle aged Mrs. Kanika Lahiri,
from SriKanta's neighboring village Taherpur, mother of Balaram,
came forward to read a few verses from her beloved *Sri Sri
Krishner Ashtottar Satanam*, 108 names of Sri Krishna, realizing
Sri Kanta was one of the names given to Krishna by His devotees.
Mrs. Lahiri was one of the very few women present at the meeting,
and perhaps it was the first political act of this grandmother.
Panchali is read by Hindu Bengalis telling how their gods and
goddesses have many meanings to people of all backgrounds and
diverse faiths to match their mood, desire and wishes. Mrs. Lahiri
remembered the long poem by heart, as she recited every
Thursday evening during Lakhsmi Puja, worshipping of Goddess
Lakshami, and on Saturday evening *puja* at her shrine at home.
This is normally read with an undulating voice, not exactly like a
song, but after listening to its melodious rendering, the rhythm
captivates the listeners as they join in its recitation giving it a
meditative effect. Though this is not a gathering where a *panchali*
can be read, but seeing no Hindu volunteer to read from the
scriptures to give the crowd moral courage, her inner spirit told
her to come forward. She was dressed like a typical Bengali
middle-aged housewife, white sari with red border, red *sindur*
(vermillion) dot on her forehead and on the parting of her scalp

showing her status as a married woman, with red *pala* coral and white conch wedding bangles on her both hands. Mrs. Lahiri covered her head with sari *ghomta* hood, with folded hands touching her forehead as if she was beginning her evening prayer, then she said a shortened form of the narration :

ননীচোরা নাম রাখে যতেক গোপিনী।   (৭)

(*NoniChora naam rakhey jateko gopini*)

Milk-maids named Him NoniChora (Cheese-thief) darling, (7)

Kala Shona (Black-gold) chosen by Radha-Binodini. (8)

....

Devotees named Him Lord of the world, our Jagannath, (61)

Durbbasa called Him orphans' dad, Lord Sri Nath. (62)

....

Manjari named Him killer of anti-work, Karma-bandha-Naash, (107)

Women of Brajaland called Him giver of wish Purna-Avilash. (108)

....

Listen dear oh my brother the name in repeat,

Curses will go away hearing it so sweet.

The names of Krishna and Hari are really delight,

One, who prays at the Krishna name, is really bright.

Then she added impromptu,

SriKanta naam rakey Mriduler nandan,

Soitan kemoney khai jay thaakey chirantan?

Name SriKanta was given to Mridul's scion

Can Satan take away if one is with his men and women?

After saying the verses Mrs. Lahiri folded her hand again touching her forehead and continued with silent meditation for a minute or two. Then there were heated discussion about writing a letter to Bangladeshi President, local Canadian parliamentarian and the head of Bangladesh Caucus in the U.S. Congress and meet in person with the foreigners to influence their home administration for arresting the murderers who were openly walking the streets still harassing rest of the tormented family. Except for a non-Bangladeshi, no one volunteered and finally the buck was passed to the newly formed Canadian Bangladeshi Minority Unity Council. After some cajoling Mr. Narendra Nath SurjoPrasad, a Bangladeshi Hindu from the small Marwari — a group living in Bangladesh for hundreds of years with origin in Western Indian state of Rajasthan, but speaking Bengali as its mother tongue, inseparable from native Hindus — community was drafted to write the letters. Mr. SurjoPrasad wrote :

H. E. President Prof. Dr. Iajuddin Ahmed

Respected Honorable President :

Re : *The Brutal Murder of Srikanta Rakshit and Prosecution of the Killers*

We are writing to you seeking justice for one of the ghastly crimes of the nation's recent past : the brutal murder of the young and talented Srikanta Rakshit, son of Advocate Sri Mridul Kanti Rakshit of Hazari Lane, Chittagong, who was beheaded and a severed body part was sent to the family as a warning to families like them. We knew Srikanta since he was a little child. All of us were looking forward for him to blossom as a promising citizen of Bangladesh. We have learned from the media in gory details that a long-time Muslim criminal is the chief instigator of the ghastly crime. We have also learned that through anti-Hindu terror of the Enemy Property Act he forcibly occupied the ancestral land and home of the Rakshit family for ethnic cleansing of that Hindu family for India, as millions of Hindus have faced similar fate. It is disturbing to learn that he and his criminal gang are still walking free. It is being reported that since the late 1990s this gang has been getting protection from influential quarters when the assets of the Rakshit family were first confiscated. It is yet hard to believe that even after the ghastly murder, Rakshits are still receiving threats. Recently the daughter of the family was targeted for persecution.

We are appealing to you to help the State prosecute the communalist killers immediately. We would also urge that the Government take immediate steps to evict the illegal occupiers, provide reparation to the family including personal damages paid by the criminals for the pain and suffering of the Rakshit family. We thank the Prime Minister for arresting some of the butchers. We wish you could bring Srikanta back.

The meeting decided to send the letter not only to the president but also to other top officials and to influential politicians of Canada and the U.S. There was discussion whether or not to send letters to the top Bangladeshi-Indian officials of the Communist Parties who run the neighboring Bengali states of West Bengal and Tripura, but that idea was dropped as at earlier attempts to reach out to them met with stone silence, and only suggestion the received was to leave their 'Muslim Bangladesh' homeland for colonization of India.

Mr. Dwijen Guha-Thakurta, a former school teacher, spoke on the issue of illegal confiscation of minority Hindu properties

through the application of Enemy Property Act, and how that
Nazi-like act has been used to take over SriKanta family's assets
of tens of generations by new settlers by declaring the original
inhabitants as 'enemies of state' for their continued belief of their
ancestral traditions, Hinduism. An act was established in the days
of open anti-Hindu racism of Pakistan when minority Hindu
properties could be taken over by Muslims by simply declaring
Hindus as the 'enemy of the state.' No reason was needed to
identify a Hindu as 'enemy of the state' and a recent Muslim migrant
could move in to a Hindu property without any notice and without
paying a penny to the Hindu. One just had to go to the local
police station and write a complaint against a Hindu, while the
victim had to go to the Supreme Court to reverse the process of
that complaint. Mr. Guha-Thakurta even cited two books on the
subject by SriKanta's lawyer father Mridul : *Law of Vested
(Enemy) Properties in Bangladesh*, Vol. I, 1985 and *Law of
Vested (Enemy) Properties*, Vol. II, 1991. 'Cruelty of the law is
that it not only takes properties away from the original inhabitants
of the land, but it declares them enemies of state,' explained the
speaker. "The Hindus, who were 90% to 95% of the 3 million
killed during the 1971 genocide in Bangladesh by the Islamic Army
of Pakistan and by Islamist Bengalis, are being called 'enemy of
the state.' The law could not' as the speaker explained 'be applied
against the Muslim killers of the Father of the Nation Mujibur
Rahman. Yet it allowed taking over of the ancestral properties of
parliamentarian Dhirendra Nath Datta, who and whose son were
abducted by Pakistan Army from their home, never to be found
again. Mrs. Protiti Devi, Mr. Datta's daughter-in-law would learn
from other survivors how her father-in-law and brother-in-law
were tortured to death while injured in the first killing attempt by
the Army of Islamic Pakistan. Mr. Datta was the first to propose
Bengali to be the national language of Pakistan, and that language

issue gave rise to the Bengali nation. It would be like calling George Washington, Mahatma Gandhi or Ho Chi Minh to be the enemies of the Unites States of America, India and Vietnam respectively.' Mr. Datta's granddaughter would end up publishing a book, *An Inquiry into Causes and Consequences of Deprivation of Hindu Minorities in Bangladesh through the Vested Property Act* (PRIP Trust, Dhaka, 2000) that would document confiscation of over 2.5 million acres of land, plus tens of thousands of homes, buildings, shops, ponds, businesses just in a short period of 1990s in the small Wisconsin-size nation. 'SriKanta was an innocent victim of that unchecked greed,' the speaker ended with tears in the eyes of all the attendees.

To the surprise of many Americans and Canadians when the atrocity against Srikanta was posted on a South Asian journalists' e-discussion forum, many of the young leftist Bangladeshi Muslims objected as this was an act not directed against Hindu minorities.[4]

Finally Aunirban Anthony stopped pacing and summoned enough courage to ring his old classmate Tofael, a Muslim, and now a top official in the district. Tofael told Aunirban that he had already heard about Theresa's abduction, and promised to do 'everything in his power,' but recommended 'Anthony to get a large ransom demand ready, because Hindus and Christians can not be given protection in this land.' Then he called Mr. Narendra Nath SurjoPrasad, writer of SriKanta's protest note, to help him draft a similar letter seeking liberation of his sister. But, it was a telephone call from the Christian Methodist minister that showed him a ray of hope, followed by a call from his headmaster. *Lakshmi-babu*, the headmaster, assured him that a large contingent of his Hindu students have gone to David home, while the Bangladesh Minority Council members are planning a day-long vigil for arrest and prosecution of the kidnappers. The

---

4. South Asian Journalist Association, U.S.A., discussion in Fall 2003.

Christian Methodist minister on the other end of the line assured
him, 'Anthony, I have called our Church hierarchy to look into
the case and liberate Theresa. They in turn are going to call the
presidents and prime ministers for prosecution of the criminals.
They have already called our Vice President's office. Let us pray
that Anjana is returned home safe, unharmed.'

Strangely Aunirban called Aunt *Mashima*, the *panchali*
reader, as if she can help him, and told her that he couldn't believe
it could happen to Christians. He couldn't stop crying. Mashima
realized that Aunirban needed a mother-like person to console
him. Mashima's son Balaram offered to be with Aunirban, 'Let
me come, I know how you feel. I too have lost my older sister.
Ma earlier told me 'we will not allow it to happen to another
family. We must do that we couldn't do when we lived back home.'
Balaram said, 'Ma asked to call all our Hindu family members
and neighbors to be with you parents. We must liberate Theresa.'

Chapter 12

Tarpan : Offering

Ajoy was trying to think when was the last he went for *tarpan*, offering for the ancestors. He was having hard time to recollect that. He has a hazy memory of a childhood occasion when he went holding his father's hand to Ganga (Ganges) in the early morning of the auspicious *Mahalaya*, the day when the countdown to the Bengali festival of Mother Goddess Durga — Durga Puja — begins, to offer water to their ancestors. *Mahalaya* is an auspicious time for *tarpan* offering. He couldn't remember whether he was five or six then. It was not far from their refugee Colony, within 'walking distance' of about 2 miles. Ajoy's father used to say that back home in their ancestral village he used to take all his children for *tarpan* at *Mahalaya*. There he used to take them to either Aatreyi River or to the huge pond named *Purono Dighi* or Old Lake adjacent to their *Thakur-bari*, or Temple-building. Since they fled their home at Dehergoti village near Netrokona they have been living at this illegal *jabar-dhakhal*, forcibly occupied, *Barendra* (Upper Bengal) Hindu Refugee Colony. In one room seven of them lived. Ma-Baba — Mom and dad, Dada — elder brother — Abhoy-charan, younger sisters Gita, Sita and the oldest son Sankar of Aunt *Chhoto-pishi*, father's younger sister. Ever since they left behind their ancestral brick-built *dalan-bari* manor of their village home, his mom and dad frequently used to bicker about leaving their ancestral home, and now living in this one-room shack. For a long time he had seen his parents weep about this. He couldn't understand why. At times he used to be angry seeing an old man weep. 'How strange for such old people to cry,' Ajoy used to think. He still remembers that during *tarpan* offering his father standing in waist-deep water didn't used to stop like others after offering water and symbolic food held in the cup of his two palms to three, five, seven or even fourteen ancestors, like others. He would try to offer up to thirty-seven or thirty-eight fore parents. Had he forgotten the names he would start again starting with his father, "Guru-charan, then grandfather Ram-charan, great-grandfather Sri-charan, Kali-charan, and so on." Sometimes father used be completely silent, tears used to roll down his eyes but he used to make sure that his children, Abhoy, Ajoy, Gita and Sita, didn't find that out, hiding in the water that was being lifted by his palms from the river. But it wasn't difficult for the children to figure that out. Years later children found out that for at least thirty-eight generations the family had taken part at Durga Puja at their village *Puja-Mandap*, festival building, and their father Shambhu-charan was possibly seeking forgiveness from their forefathers for not being able to continue that tradition.

Gradually privileged and oppressed caste Hindu Ghosh, Datta, Nandi, Munshi, Sarkar, Dey, Sengupta, Das, Kulu, Khatua, Guha and Christian Gomes families vanished from the village. Rich, middle-class, poor, dirt-poor, teacher, shopkeeper, businessmen, *Dhopa* washer men, *Napit* barber. From these fleeing refugees they used to get bits of news from their village and used to dream of their return. Moreover, Ajoy's mother used to get news of the village for her close friend and a neighbuor Mrs. Meherunnechha Biswas, a Muslim, whose nickname was Chhani, and the children called her *Chhani-pishi* or Aunt Chhani, father's sister. For some years *Selima-boudi*, sister-in-law Selima, a Muslim, of the *jotdar*, a large landlord, family also used to write to Ajoy's mother. That stopped. A while back Chhani-pishi, wrote to mother, "Didi," older sister, "this year there was no Puja. *Thakur-kaka*, the priest uncle, came to the *Puja-Mandap*, festival building, every day and practically guarded the place. He lit earthen *pradip* lamp each day. On *Shashti*, sixth day of the moon and the first day of Durga Puja, I bathed early morning at the pond, then left flowers and *bel* leaves[1] at the *mandap* platform where the deity used to be kept. Then I thought about you, after I prayed (Muslim) *namaz*. Village with out the sounds of *dhak* drum, I could never think about it! I couldn't sleep for days, I continuously shed tears. But, no one at home knows about it............" People at Ajoy's home cried too after receiving that letter. Thereafter, within a day or two, Mr. Shambhu-charan had a heart attack.

Chhani-pishi used to write to Ajoy's Ma on special occasions like Hindu festivals of Durga Puja, *Bijoya* — the time to exchange greetings, Muslim festival of *Id*, and during Bengali *Nababarsha* New Year in mid-April. Ajoy used to be amused as both of them addressed each other as '*Didi*' or older sister, a Bengali tradition. From the letters of Chhani-pishi mother came to know of the end of the Puja festival, and that thereafter the poor, mostly oppressed caste Hindu families of Rai, Haldar, Barman, Saha, Gayen, Kishku, and Muslim families of Daud and Kaiser used to leave offerings of flower besides a water-filled earthen *ghat* pitcher[2] at the *mandap* festival platform each year during festivals. She also learned that in most of the time it was *Thakur-kaka*, uncle priest, used to decorate the *mandap* platform, Chatterji *Thakurma* (Grandma) of an erstwhile Brahmin family used to *Bisarjan* immerse the *ghot* pitcher at the end of their imaginary festivity, and Ghorami *Bouma*, wife of the oppressed caste Hindu Ghorami family, used to carry the offered flowers and *bel* leaves for *bisarjan* immersion. Once the youngest housewife Farida of the rich Muslim family brought a *dhaki*, *dhak* drum player, during one of the Durga

---

1. Leaves from *bel*, wood-apple, tree are considered sacred and assential for Hindu worship services.

2. In the absence of beautifully sculptured and decorated deities, poor families or for unusual circumstances water-filled *ghat* pitcher is used as a substitute for deities. In any case, water-filled pitchers are needed for those services.

Puja festival days, and joined with Chatterji *Thakurma* Grandma
for immersion of the pitcher. This became a huge scandal in the
village, and many threatened *Thakurma* to leave the village
immediately, or else! From her letter mother came to know of
'missing' of the youngest daughter Durga, the little goddess of the
family of *Thukur-kaka*, Uncle Priest, to the local young Muslim
mastan gangs, and in sorrow the subsequent death of Aunt
Kakima, *Thakur-kaka's* wife. And of the news of Nandi family
taking their daughter Sumitra to Dhubri in Assam state in India to
find her a suitable match there, and of their son Chaitanya becoming
a monk *sanyasi* at an ashram at Gopalgonj, in Bangladesh and
finally *Thakur-kaka* taking the role of the protector of Puja
building. Ma-Baba, mom and dad, used to look for news about
their home which Aunt *Pishi* never wrote.

From that time folks of Dehergoti village were planning to
organize a puja festival of the Dehergoti *Sammelani* (association),
as there were thousands of such village-based pujas in India among
refugee groups. It is said that to arrange a Durga Puja there needs
lakhs, tens of thousands, of discussion and the help of thousands
of hands. There are lots of expenses too. All of the folks are in
pitiable condition. Still, people have decided this time around they
would have 'Dehergoti Puja' in Calcutta. After a large-scale anti-
Hindu disturbance last year in and around the village, many of
poor, oppressed caste Hindu *kumar* potters, *dhaki* drum players,
moira sweet makers, and others had fled to India. The taxi driver
son of Kundu family, Shuvo, has pledged most of the sums needed
for the festival. It was decided that they would observe only three
days instead of five of Durga Puja, *Ashtami, Nabami* and
Dasami, the eighth, ninth and the tenth days respectively of the
moon. But, everyone also came to realize that to make the festival
a success they must have the soil from their *Puja Mandap* festival
building area and the water of Aatryei River or that of their *Purono*

Dighi pond, "which are needed even more than Holy Ganga water." And they need *Thakur-kaka*, Uncle Priest. Narayan Ghosh who used to be lovingly called *Thanku-kaka*, *Dome-thakur* — Priest of Cremation Undertaker, *Shiv-thakur* — God of Forgiveness, and with many other names. For generations his family had served the local residents, and a big tension had developed of the merits of a puja without his presence. Mr. Ghose belonged to an oppressed-caste poor peasant family, and supports themselves with earnings from bamboo handicrafts.

Like most young people of his age and friends circle, Ajoy never took part in Hindu *Tarpan* or puja celebrations. Suddenly two days before Mahalaya, Ajoy's pregnant wife Minati called her mother-in-law to show her a note from Ajoy:

"I am going to Dehergoti. Don't worry about me. I'll return timely with soil and water. Please look after your health......."

In the early hours of Ashtami, the eighth day of the moon, *Kamini-debi*, Mrs. Kamini, Ajoy's mother, heard a knock on the door. "Ma, look who is here."

Opening the door, she found *Thakur-kaka* with Ajoy. Before *Kamini-debi* could say anything, *Thakur-kaka* Uncle said the first words, "*Barro Bouthan*, Oldest Wife of the Family, I came here at the invitation of Ma Durga." In excitement and joy tears flowed of Kamini's eyes. Almost everyone in the house was awake in that early morning for making puja arrangements, and for the new life to join the family.

Ajoy's mom tried to bring her composure back, and called for the rest of the family.

"Hey, all of you children, daughter, son-in-law, and rest of the crowd please come right away. Ajoy has brought along *Bhagaban*, God, Narayan, Himself in to this Earth. Please offer your *pranam* respect." She continued, "Ma Durga has already arrived at our home. Let's show her to Uncle Narayan (God)."

Mrs. Kamini told her *Kaka-babu*, Uncle Kaka, "This time we won't let you slip from us. You're not young any more. Even if this is not the perfect place, please stay here with us permanently. I never thought that I'll see you again."

With his big laugh *Narayan-babu* reminded them, "Now I have three (incarnations of) Goddess Durga. But, my Durgas are still waiting for me back home." After distributing gifts of 'Puja Sweets' made by himself, he invited everyone, "Come, let's visit your Ganga. Back home we went to the river on Mahalaya day. I'll have *mukti*, liberation, after a dip in your Ganga." And for the liberation of his *Dadu* Grandpa, Narayan Ghosh, Ajoy started remembering the names, 'Shambhu-charan, Guru-charan, Ram-charan, Sri-charan........'

Chapter 13
The Crossing

In the old days in Bengal, an area that covers the world's largest delta, for people to go from one village to another, from home to distant lands, one's principal mode of travel had to be either dinghy or big boat. This water transport may have been the only mode of travel. The ox-drawn carts and palanquin used in land transportation had to stop at ferries to cross numerous rivers, streams and canals crisscrossing the land. Paved roads and bridges are relatively new invention. That's why one of Bengal and India's noted poets wrote awhile ago:

'Who wants to cross, Oh my merry?

Waiting by the water's edge, by my ferry..........'

This is jet age. So most of the travel from country to country, takes place by airplane. I've heard from my parents, grandparents and uncles and aunts that in the old pre-partition days they used to travel from Calcutta in West Bengal to Dhaka, Khulna, Barisal, Chandpur, Goalando, Chittagong in Bangladesh, then East Bengal, and even Rangoon (Yangon) in Burma (Myanmar), by steamer, launch and ship. With India's independence and subsequent partition of Bengal 'the sun has set and the gentle bridge has stopped blowing,' as the poet wrote in a different context, those water routes cease to exist as barriers and unresponsive bureaucracies developed. However, in Europe the ferry system is still competing with jet planes. Among those services that I've enjoyed immensely are the England-France, Ireland-Wales, Scotland-Northern Ireland, Germany-Denmark, Denmark-Sweden, and Norway-Denmark rides. Whenever I boarded those ferries it reminded me of the riverine Bangladesh. At one time in the history of India one could travel from Calcutta to Kashi

(Varanasi), Patna, Allahabad following Ganga River and to Puri and Madras, by boat.

First time ever I crossed a national boundary was by air. Afterwards my family crossed U.S.-Canada border several times, mostly by car. Once from Upstate New York we went to Montreal, Quebec for a few hours for a dinner. Similarly we once went to Belgium from the Netherlands just for dinner. I crossed other land borders between U.S. and Mexico, and among European and Central Asian nations. First time I crossed a national boundary was in early seventies. Before that in the sixties I went to Benapole, then West Bengal-East Pakistan (now Bangladesh) border crossing with my friend Pijush. Pijush joined our Engineering & Architecture College from East Pakistan all of a sudden, in the middle of the 5-year degree program that was extremely unusual as all the students were only admitted in the first year through a competitive exam. He was admitted either in the 2nd or 3rd year. Besides, there were Shesadri, Soumitra, Anjan, Prosanta, Shivaprosad and may be a few others, all Hindus from the Muslim-majority land. In 1964 a rumor was floated in East Pakistan that the Holy Hair of Prophet Hazrat Mohammad, the Founder of Islam, was stolen from the Hazrat Bal (Hair) Mosque of Srinagar City in the distant Jammu and Kashmir state of North India unleashing a rein of terror, a pogrom, by the Federal Pakistan and Provincial East Pakistan Governments on Hindus of East Pakistan. As a result it was estimated that over 10,000 non-Muslim Hindus were killed, and more than 1.2 million Hindus, Buddhists, tribals sought refuge in India.[1] This was the official government estimate

---

1. See, daily Bengali *Ittefaque* of Dhaka, Bangladesh [East Pakistan], 15 January 1964; London *Times*, 23 January 1964; and *Washington Post*, 22 January 1964; and recently it was written about in the Bengali daily *Bhorer Kagoz* of Dhaka, Bangladesh, 8 November 1990. And for the estimation of Hindu refugee see by Marcus Franda in *Population Politics in South Asia*, American University, 1972.

of refugee. Among these refugees were a number of brilliant engineering, architecture, medical and other college students. Pijush and the others were in that group. On the first day of the pogrom, Pijush's home was attacked. His father was a renowned physician. The plan was to teach his father Gouri-Shankar 'a lesson' after attacking his home and destroying his medical office. They wanted to imprison both father and son, may be murder them. Pijush hid himself in a pond under *shapla* lily. After beating his mother and father black and blue, police took the father away. When her mother protested carrying her husband away, she was further beaten up and humiliated by their Muslim neighbors. After that event Pijush's parents wanted him to flee. He fled to Assam state in India along with his friends and relations, but not his parents. After staying in a refugee camp for sometime, he joined another refugee camp in West Bengal. From there after pleading at many places, he was admitted to our college by a special order of the ruling Congress Party-run State Government. Back home as his mother's health deteriorated, his Mama Uncle, mother's brother, admitted her to a hospital. After a few months, when her condition became a bit stable, at her husband's urging she came to Calcutta for treatment after receiving a Pakistani passport and an Indian visa. A year later, after the 1965 Pakistan-India war, all India-East Pakistan connections were severed, cutting his mother, Aditi-debi, Mrs. Aditi, off from her husband. Finally, Aditidebi came to know through a postcard from her brother Joydev that the distance with her husband would never be bridged in this life. When the situation became 'a bit normal' Aditidebi was rushing back at the first opportunity to overcome her grief of not being 'able to offer her husband water in his mouth before his soul left the body,' a pious duty of all Hindus, especially of the loved ones. When she went to Calcutta at the advice of Gouri-babu, Mr. Gouri, her husband, she traveled by removing her wedding *sankha* conch bracelets and *sindur* vermilion mark on her scalp lest Muslims find out her religion. And now she was returning back to her husband's home breaking her wedding conch bangles and washing off the *sindur* from her scalp as a widow. At the border crossing Pijus told, "Be careful Ma." But mother replied, "What am I afraid of now?" This time mother was traveling alone by herself, on the other side was standing Pijush's Mama maternal uncle. At the village home Mama Uncle used to wear *dhuti* outfit, but as during the pogrom many '*dhuti*-clad' were killed — as it identified them as Hindu or Buddhist — this time he wore white *fotua* shirt and white *pajama*. The check post was deserted. As long as we were there, Pijush's Ma was the only person to cross the border. At first we waived our hand from a distance to signal of our arrival. Then with the permission and pity of the border guards we advanced in small steps to the white line on the road surface indicating the separation of the divided nation. On top of the white line was the iron pole barrier preventing vehicular traffic. We the people of one country touched the feet of the people of another country. Pijush's mother became a foreigner, legally. Though Pijush wanted to be a citizen of his homeland, but his homeland wouldn't allow him to be part of his nation. In spite of best efforts Pijush could not get a passport of his homeland. In tears Aditidebi tried to console her son, then moved forward in tiny steps. With teary eyes Pijush also tried consoling her mother from this side of the white line, standing next to that iron barrier was the foreign son of a *desi* native mother! Gradually *Mahsi* Aunt's white *thaan* sari of the widows and Mama Uncle's white pajama and white *fotua* became hazier and hazier.

Afterwards I have crossed this land border many times. The first time I crossed the border I traveled westward from Bangladesh to West Bengal, India. On this trip we found Mr. Mokbul Hasan, a *bonedi* aristocratic Muslim from North Calcutta, as our companion from Jessore City, 75 miles north of the border to the Benapole crossing. Mr. Hasan arranged for his daughter Afroza to marry a very suitable Tareq of Dhaka, Bangladesh, where both the newlyweds were living. He went to Dhaka to bring Tareq and Afroza to Calcutta, India for the couple to live permanently. "Who wants to live in that *mlechho* Muslim land?" A Muslim Hasan used an unused mlechho, dirty or foreign, sometimes used as a slur on Muslim and European cow-eating foreigners.

A few days ago, this time on an eastward journey, I crossed Benapole from the West Bengal side heading to Bangladesh. I took a very early morning 30 US cents (40 mile) commuter train from Calcutta, before sunrise, a young Abul Fazal Ahmed of Hughly, north of Calcutta, was my companion — a stranger I met at the platform, as you often do on your travel in India. A simple-looking Abul sought me out as *Kaku* (Uncle) for possible protection from the extortionists at the border, who often ignore *bhadralok* (gentlemen). He was going to his aunt's house at Chittagong in Bangladesh with a heavy heart leaving behind his mother, brother and brother's wife behind, heading to an even poorer country, but majority with his own religion. It was the Muslim fasting month of Ramzan. There he was to attend the Muslim *Kulkhani* memorial ceremony at his *Pishi* Aunt, father's sister. Then he would head to Saudi Arabia with a Bangladeshi passport. He could not find such opportunities in Calcutta. "*Janani janmabhumischa swargadapi gariyashee*, Mother and Motherland are even better than Heaven," Abul said a common Sanskrit proverb used in everyday Bengali, "so it is quite natural for me to feel so sad." But the sadness was overshadowed by the inhuman treatment of the customs and immigration officials. Abul and I were together till immigration where we were separated because of our different passports. Thereafter we had to stand in two separate lines. When we met again, Abul said, "*Kaku* (Uncle), having had an Indian passport Indians took less bribe, but the Bangladesh officials took three times that." This was the norm. One gentleman informed that he had to pay twelve hundred takas (rupees) to two sides. A highly respected Calcutta personality once told me a visitor "Do you know how much each individual of an official Bangladeshi delegation coming to India through a Government invitation had to pay (bribe) at the border crossing?" A friend from Dhaka echoed the same. Said 'Birds of the same feather,' using a Bengali metaphor, 'Thieves behave like they're maternal cousins!' I could not find a single soul crossing the border who wasn't displeased at the crossing, yet their horror washed away quickly by seeing the loved ones on the other side.

Once I took the Darshana-Gede, Bangladesh-West Bengal (India) 'Check Post' border crossing where in the absence of even a dirt path one has to walk along a railway track. If one wants to know what disasters that might result in partitioning of a nation brought through the efforts of politicians, one must pay a visit to places like Gede-Darshana crossing. But, that is a separate issue. In these crossings the harassment that individuals go through for traveling legally by having a passport and visa, is beyond description. I witnessed at Gede in West Bengal forcible illegal confiscation of the last currency from the pocket of a sick Hindu gentleman heading to Calcutta for treatment. And at Darshana in Bangladesh a resident informed me that he goes "regularly to Calcutta illegally almost like a daily passenger (commuter)" known locally as 'Number Two' method of border crossing, *i.e.*, without any visa or passport. On one of my trips when I crossed the Akhaura 'Check Post' border crossing between Tripura in Northeast India and eastern Bangladesh, I was the fourth traveler for my eastward journey from Bangladesh to Tripura, but was number one when returning to Bangladesh at about

3 PM in the afternoon.[2] From Bangladesh the legal route towards Akhaura crossing bordering capital city of Agartala of Tripura is the straight surfaced road. While the illegal Number Two or free-market crossing is through the two dirt roads taking travelers to either sides of the legal crossing. Both at nearby Bangladeshi border city of Comilla and at Agartala, Tripura, it was suggested by the 'touts,' the illegal people movers, that "they would deliver to the other side at lower cost, in less time and with much ease." It was not difficult to figure out looking at the empty road of one route while traffic jams at other two whether bureaucracy or free market was winning the confidence of the people. On the latest trip while crossing the white line at the Benapole border Pijush came to my mind again. Time, has changed, so have the nations. With the rise in economic and political relation Benapole has become the biggest land port of the two nations. Though the border crossings have not became as easy as it is in Europe, Africa and the Americas, it has improved a lot nonetheless in the last 30 years, leaving aside the illegal trafficking. I hope the crossings will become easier. Before I left for Bangladesh on my last visit, Dilip, a classmate of Pijush said, "you must meet Pijush at Sylhet. He has gone there from India and his wife Indira and their children to celebrate his fathers' hundredth birthday. He has gone through the same Benapole crossing, taking with him a lump of the soil of Benapole, then East Pakistan, now Bangladesh, which he collected with you when you saw his mother off leaving India for their homeland."

---

2. In Bangladesh as well as in India the officials make hand written entries with each traveler recorded numerically each day with #1 being the first one.

Chapter 14

Our Sacred Tradition of Putting Nature First[1]

We Bengalis are very creative. We take to singing from birth to death, while rowing boats and harvesting; we dance welcoming newlyweds and new year; we take to overnight poetry, theological discourse, *tablighi*, *jalsha*, *pala*, *jatra*, *matua* and *kirtan*. Our Rap music in the form of *kabigan* has been with us for centuries, as has been getting elevated with ganja on high holydays to contemplate abstract forms. Gopal Bhar reminds us of our sense of humor at our own cost showing self-confidence.

One of the important areas of study of overseas scholars has been our religion, especially Vaishnavism and nature-worshipping Hinduism in association with our now-200 million Bengali gods and goddess. Yes, 200 million now ! And the synthesis of Bengali Hinduism, Bengali Vaishnavism, Bengali Islam and Bengali Buddhism has also been of great interest to others. Bengali devotion to Goddess of Strength Ma Kali, teachings of Raja Ram Mohon, Sri Ramakrishna, Sri Aurobindo, *puthi* and Rabindranath were also of interest to many scholars, but the importance of nature in the Bengali mind interested a large section of scholars: our tradition of putting nature first. We worship our soil, our rivers and ponds, our animals, plants, flowers and fauna. They are all sacred to us. Remember, বাংলার মাটি বাংলার জল পূণ্য হউক, পূণ্য হউক হে ভগবান (Let Bengal's soil, Bengal's water be blessed, Oh Dear God?) Or, Kazi Nazrul Islam tells us in his own style, এই সুন্দর ফুল সুন্দর ফল, মিঠা নদীর পানি, খোদা তোমার মেহেরবাণি। এই শস্য শ্যামল ফসল ভরা মাটির ডালি খানি, খোদা তোমার মেহেরবাণি। (These beautiful flowers, fine flowing waters, God it is Your blessing. This earthen basket

1. Based on Keynote Speech at the 37th Bengal Studies Conference, Stamford University, Dhaka, Bangladesh, January 4-6, 2005.

full of creation and food, God it is Your blessing). Those of you who love Ramprasadi songs of Mother of Creation would recognize his way of giving thanks to nature, জগতকে খাওয়াচ্ছেন যে মা, সুমধুর খাদ্য নানা / ওরে কোন লাজে খাওয়াতে চাস্ তাঁয়, আলো চাল আর মুগ ভিজানো । (The Mother is feeding the universe; delicious food for all of us But why do you shamelessly offer Her only coarse rice and wet lentils?). Living in the world's largest delta fish too is sacred, and special. Marriages could not take place until we send gifts of fish as *tatwa* to the other family; it can not be held without welcoming the newlyweds with our sacred soil, water, grass and grains. Even in our baby's *Annaprasan*, first rice eating or going into solid in Western terminology, a fish has to bless the decorated plate. With the rise of monotheistic Islam and atheism some of these traditions have been lost or are severely frayed, just as modernity, Westernization, Anglicization, Marxism, Christianity and urbanization all have taken its toll on our age-old tradition in both Bangladesh and West Bengal. This is logical, except when done by intolerant political force. This is understandable. But many more of those tradition still survive. Our ancestors appropriated secular partnerships with nature as thier own, just as many Hindus have appropriated Muslim *pirs*, Buddhist gurus or Christian mothers as their own. In our Bengal for a long time Muslims too have appropriated many Hindu deities and Hindu sages. Yet in modern Arabized Islam there were not much room for celebrating evolution from our wet and evergreen beauty. Growing up in a city I could never realize why on earth sale of plants and animals take place during Chariot Festival of Lord Jagannath, *Rather-mela* festivities, in the monsoon month of Bhadra (mid-August to mid-September) until a *Bedey*, a Bengali gypsy, saleswoman reminded me that plants and animals have a better chance of survival in the life-giving rainy season, *pacha* (rotten) *Bhadra*. After a bitter cold, spring is life giving in Europe and America just as monsoon brings life to the Indian Subcontinent after our sizzling summer. Similar nature-human symbiosis exists between *pitha-payesh* (pan cakes and rice pudding) and *Poush-Sankranti* (end of the winter month of Poush) celebrations. Who can think of that wonderful festivity withour *khejurer-rosh* (date palm drink) and *khejur gur* (date molasses), products of Bengali winter?

Our love of nature created many taboos and traditions in our society in order to create a harmony between us with the Mother Nature. Some of those nature-protecting traditions are already gone. At one stage in my life I too championed breaking our traditions. Now I realize breaking something for breaking sake is not good enough. Something good must replace that. There are many examples I could cite, but let me mention one of our nature-related taboos from our coastal Bangladeshi tradition that I diligently broke which I now realize had real purpose: it is not eating *ilish macch* (shad-like hilsa fish) from Kali Puja in the Bengali/Indian month of Kartik (mid-October through mid-November) to Saraswati Puja in Magh (mid-January through mid-February). At Kali Puja we would have sad face thinking about the days without *ilish*. There would be special prayers for a bigger harvest the upcoming season. During Saraswati Puja we were to bring a pair of *ilish* as precious trophy, decorate with *sindur*, *pan* and jewelry as something very dear, very human. The real reason we didn't eat *ilish* during that period as it was the time of spawning, but the skeptic in me did not accept my parents' rationale then. A few years ago as I was invited to an agriculture cooperative in eastern Bangladesh, I was presented with a poster that still hangs in our basement, '*jatka dhorben na:*' don't kill baby *ilish*. Fishermen explained how the annual catch has dropped in that area as we take more and more baby fish, and suggested that we will be better off by making that taboo as our law. No wonder nature-inspired Khanar Bachan (Words of Khana, a learned lady of ancient times) has had such an influence in rural Bengal. In some areas of the West as they broke taboos of the nature-loving, nature-worshiping natives, they wiped out many species of plants and animals. Now they have enacted stringent laws, making taboos legal. Near our home in New York when we go fishing in the Long Island Bay we have to release our catch immediately if that didn't measure certain length, depending on the month. This law is enforced with huge fines. Similar laws now exist in salmon fishing, deer, duck and buffalo hunting, tree cutting and more. On a recent trip to Antarctica we were reminded by our leader that by 1950s European whalers wiped out 95% of the whales in the southern oceans, as no humans in the Southern Hemisphere elevated marine mammals into something sacred, actually no humans lived in the Antarctic and in nearby islands. In the north, near Arctic, where humans lived the Eskimos and Inuits considered whales, sea lions and seals as sacred and developed taboos when not to kill or how and when to kill. Their lives depended on these animals. But European colonization disregarded those taboos, until they imposed them as new laws to prevent extinction of those animals.

In traditional agrarian Bengal our lives revolve around Mother Nature, and we developed *baaro mashey tayro parbon :* 13 festivities in 12 months.[2] Our gratitude to nature was expressed eloquently by Dwijendra Lal Roy :

ধন ধান্য পুষ্প ভরা আমাদের এই বসুন্ধরা

তাহার মাঝে আছে দেশ এক সকল দেশের সেরা ।।

(The land full of flowers, wealth and grain,

---

2. As traditional Islamic holydays do not match with Bengali seasons and as the holydays move each year, they haven't created festivities associated with seasonal gifts of Mother Nature. Exceptions to these are many festivities with our own Islamic *pirs* (saints) and at Muslim *dargahs* (mausoleums).

This is the best country amongst all the countries.

This is the best land among all the terrain.)

From *Nabanno* (harvest festival in fall) to *Poush Shankranti* (end of a winter *Poush* month) to *Chaitra Sankranti* (end of the hot spring month of *Chaitra*) to *Rawther Mela* (chariot festival) to *Dole* (spring festival of colors) to *Baisakhi Mela* (fair of the first month of the year, *Baisakh*, mid-April to mid-May) to festivals with snakes at *Nag Panchami* are connected with celebrating something with the nature. As all these festivals are on different seasons, their celebrations are also associated with flowers, fruits and products of the season. It gave those seasonal products, including animal life, additional sacred protection. Our new Bangladeshi festivals of Bijoy Dibash (Victory Day, December 16), Ekushey (21st February Language Martyr's Day), Swadhinata Dibash (Independence Day in March), and new Paschim Bangla (West Bengal) festivals of Prajatantra (Indian Republic Day in January) and Swadhinata Dibash (Indian Independence Day in August) add to those old festivals, *parbons*. Most of us living in urban areas do not have much use for the rural-based nature-loving traditions. True. And traditions must change. True. We do not live in a frozen time period. We must grow, change or die. Also true. What we all are trying is for a balance yet progress. If the festive tradition that we have developed around Ekushey, or the varieties of *pithas* I was offered during one of my home visits on Poush Sankranti, I am more than hopeful that we will keep respecting our nature and have a future to look forward to.

Chapter 15

There Is No God, But One God

When Mishti Mashi died, her '*Neejer Lok*' or Own People as people who were closed to her were colloquially known, didn't know what to do with her dead body. The problem was neither with Mishti Mashi nor with her Own People; normally cremating the departed to return to Mother Earth was all that was needed according to Hindu custom, but poor, unlettered maid-cum-surrogate parents Mr. & Mrs. Chandra Nath & Urbashi Rajbhor created a hullabaloo about turning their mother into ashes. 'We want to bury her, keep her in eternal Samadhi at her homestead' was their uncompromising demand. Mishti Mashi literally means Sweet Aunt and she became 'a sweet mother' to all the peoples — Muslim, Hindu and Buddhist, Bengali, Manipuri and Chakma — although she was a devout Bengali Hindu. Yet hardly anyone knew their mother's real name, InduBala AgniBeena Dasi. That is the result of local tradition. No one in right mind calls an older person in Bengal by her/his first name. Even uttering the first name in association with uncle, aunt or *dada* or *didi* — older brother or sister-is considered uncourteous, thus the custom of using neutral terms like *mishti* or sweet or *sundar* (nice) or *golap* (rose) and so on. In her MollaHati village till his death while in his eighties, her middle older brother Sejda, was the last person to call her Beena or at times Indu when calling affectionately as if he was inviting her little sister to jump into the pond during summer heat. No one has heard those names since then. After the death of her Sejda, no one in MollaHati was sure of her age, and her date of birth. With her age she also came to be known as Mishti-Thakurma or Mishti-Deeda, both meaning Sweet Grandma to the children of the village, whiles ChandraNath, Urbashi and their friends, called Mishti Mashi as Barro Ma or Senior Mother, and for some reason chose 2nd Kartik, the fall month of festivity, to celebrate her birthday. Before her son Nayan and daughter-in-law Malini and their children, arrived from Khepupara in two days, it was her Own People who ferociously protected Barro Ma's lifeless body, from rotting and simultaneously resisting pressures from wealthy and influential *matabbar* individuals for cremation. In this fight ChandraNath and Urbashi were joined by Mrs. Radhika Goala the milkwoman, Muslim vegetable vendors Mr. and Mrs. Shamsher Shujohn Mia and Fazitul Jaya Begum, the Buddhist-tribal laundryman Hridoy Bikash Chakma, Manipuri *Jajmani* family priest Ananta Singha, fishermen-cum-fish seller Nanda Gopal Mridha and Mohammad Nasim Iqbal, field hands Mr. UmaKanta Mata and Mrs. Jayasri Ghosh, both Hindus, and Kalimuddin Haldar, a Muslim. It was these Own People who knew Barro Ma's last wish that she thought couldn't be carried out because she would be breaking a Hindu tradition in her Muslim-majority home. In the moments before Barro Ma breathed her last breath it was Urbashi who gave her the last drink of water, an extremely Hindu pious act, followed by other women, Hridoy's wife Ajanta and Muslim Fazitul Jaya, and men like Hridoy and ChandraNath, who spent the night at her bedside. As the situation deteriorated Urbashi summoned her husband ChandraNath in the middle of the night to call others of Own People to be with their mother; and decided to send Ananta before sunrise to catch the first bus and then ferry to Galachipa for Khepupara to bring Nayan's family back. They were hoping against hope that Barro Ma would survive the present crisis, as she had done earlier, still Ananta left a jug full of sacred water in case they needed it. The decision to send Ananta was tactical one: if Barro Ma passes away these poor, marginalized folks would tell the wealthy, influential individuals that they can't do the last rites without the family priest, and without Nayan and his family. Everyone pulled their resources to pay for bus and launch tickets. As the sun pierced its first rays through the trees surrounding the homestead, Urbashi, Ajanta and ChandraNath lifted Barro Ma up to face the Sun God bringing the warmth and light to the world, as she had done all her life. Strangely Barro Ma raised her hands from what otherwise looked like a deep coma minutes before, folded her hand and whispered 'OM Mother, please accept me in your lap,' and breathed her last breath. Normally other neighbors would have found this death instantly with women and men loudly wailing, but all of Barro Ma's Own People practically Plunging into her body with the cries absorbed by women's sari and men's gamchha towel. It was practically noiseless cry — a first for MollaHati. They all wanted to keep this a secret until Anata and Nayan returns, while crying continued ceaselessly.

All the families providing immediate vigil were poor, mostly unlettered or with grade school education, belonging to the traditionally oppressed castes or tribes. Mishti Mashi's family was known as 'Master Paribar' or teacher's family having been in teaching profession for tens of generations. In tradition-bound Indian Subcontinent this is how families specialized in various professions. One or more members of Das family were engaged in teaching in the local post-colonial British-influenced school, Adhir and Chapala Chandra Das Ingraji (English) Uccha (High) Bidyaloi (School), started in 1887 by the ancestors of Das family, grandsons of Adhir and Chapala, with the spread of 'English' education in Colonial India. Simultaneously the family continued to run their traditional Bangeswari *Toll* school until it abruptly ended with the murder of her husband Gouranga, the sole teacher of the *toll*. The toll was in existence, according to oral historians, for at least past 500 years, giving lessons to poor and rich, Hindu and Muslim. Although *toll* meant Hindu schooling, in reality it covered traditional and ancient Bengali and Sanskrit literature, thus it came to be known as Hindu schooling. Tolls also taught math, language, social science and history. Quite a few Hindus and Muslims have gone on to higher places, far and near, after graduating from Bangeswari, meaning the Goddess of Bengal. Mr. Gouranga Das taught at the local 'English' school during the day, while running the toll for an hour and a half at sunrise, which until his last breath had Hindu, Muslims and Buddhist students. Since mid-1970's, with the rise of political Islamism in his Muslim-majority homeland, there were occasional threats on the family for continuing to provide secular education to Muslims, and to relinquish their homestead to influential Muslims either free of charge or for nominal sum and flee to India. At the time of India and Bengal partition in 1947 the entire village was populated by Das clan, some connected to each other 10 or 15 or 20 generations back. As there is a taboo amongst Hindus not to marry within the 'family' thus there was hardly a marriage within the village, as they were 'related.' After successive anti-Hindu pogroms, torching of homes and attack on girls, only a handful of Dases were left at MollaHati. No one was sure why an all-Hindu village was called MollaHati meaning weekly 'market of the Islamic *molla* preacher.' One legend has it that many generations ago an Islamic preacher, *molla*, came to visit their village on a weekly *haat* market. The Dases played host to that preacher and asked him to bless their Bangeswari village *haat* market, and after that the both the village and the weekly market gradually came to be known as MollaHati, weekly market of the Islamic preacher.

Bangeswari Toll was popular among local families for another reason : it provided free tuition to needy students as well as free room and board to needy students going to public schools. For generations Das family took in half a dozen students as boarders, free of charge, from the needy families: no class, caste, religious or tribal distinction was made. They all lived together and ate the same food cooked by Mrs. Das, before that her mother-in-law, and before that her mother. For some time children of

11

ChandraNath-Urbashi, Shamsher-Fazitul, Ananta and Nanda all lived at Das home. There were two rooms at the front part of the sprawling extended family structures where the boys called 'students' lived. Girls, if there were any, lived with the family girls in the interior rooms, inseparable from the rest of the family. In these homesteads of indigenous families, over centuries people added rooms in various parts of the land as families grew larger or as new need a rose. While living with the family the girls helped other girls of the family in kitchen-related chores, while the boys helped in running errands and entertaining streams of visitors that came without notice at all hours of the day and night. Many strangers spent nights too. Dases followed Vaishnav pacifist tradition, and each morning Mr. Das would appear in the family puja shrine room leading a brief chant from holy Bhagabat Gita followed by a devotional song, while in the evening the prayer was led by the senior most lady of the house, followed by singing as time permitted. It was not necessary for students, or for that matter the members of the family, to attend these prayers but all of them generally attended except for those busy in chores. It was a time everyone looked forward to, especially the evening prayer, as this was a time they saw each other. Family and friends enjoyed singing aloud and after songs people hung around waiting for the blessed prasad food to be served while updating their day's activity.

Mishti Mashi's simple last whish was that she be buried, not cremated. 'I want to die here. I want to be part of the land forever. I want to personify the bodies of my family and Purbasha,' she would often say to her Own People. It was not much different from Guru Dasi Debi of Kapil Muni village in southwest Bangladesh who expressed 'I want to be buried here so that one day people would know that my family and I lived here, walked the path and gave our lives for Bangladesh's independence. Otherwise if I am turned into ashes, no one will remember my family.' Debi expressed this to the award-winning film director Yasmin Kabir in her film on mass rape by the Army of Islamic Republic of Pakistan and its Bengali Islamist allies, 'Independence : A Certain Liberation.' The film was based on Devi's life who was tortured for months by the Islamist soldiers after murdering her husband and minor children. She was liberated after Bangladesh's liberation, and in 2005 was living with a Muslim family, her Own People. This was a wish Mishti Mashi developed as she came out of a coma after an organized attack to kill the entire family and take over their land and other assets by local Muslim leaders. She gained her consciousness eight days after the attack which took the lives of her husband and four children. Nayan was saved as he hadn't arrived yet from his college dormitory in Dhaka. Mishti Mashi was beaten, abused and set on fire, but survived miraculously. No one knew how, but the locals said she had strong will to face her family's killers, and 'by the grace of Mother Kali.' In Bengal, as in rest of the Indian Subcontinent, rape is an 'R' word. No one wants to utter that word. People often say, 'It is better to die than be raped.' Not only the victims but often her father or older brothers commit suicide in guilt. Thus even in the court case that was filed for the Das family against the murderers, that R word was never used. Killers thought that she would die, leaving no eyewitness to the killings, 'but she had a will to live,' as Mishti Mashi's Own People would say. As she gained her consciousness, her first words were, 'Are they all right?' and after countless sedatives, many bold face lies from her suffering son, brother Sejda, the extended family, and her Own People, she gradually realized that she wont ever see them again. On the very first day at home from hospital she wanted to touch their graves, but alas there was no such thing for Hindus. Her husband's Hindu school colleagues, Mrs. Sarada Manna and Mr. Biswajit Guha Rai, sadly reminded Mishti Mashi that Hindus have no memory of their past, it is only in their myth that they dwell on, and 'they don't know even how to grieve. This is less than human for such a humanizing religion.' Fortunately son Nayan saved some of the ashes before it was immersed into the nearby Bhairab River in an earthen *ghoti* pot from the mass funeral pyre that consumed six lives, including a girl student Purbasha Satpati who was living with the family. The family and neighbors made a small 3 feet high temple-like brick shrine next to the *tulshi*-plant pedestal at the entrance of the building that adorns many Hindu homes. Once Mishti Mashi was able to reach the shrine she would talk to it for hours, offered it food before she ate just as all mothers do, offered it blessed fruits and *batasa* candy after she had offered that to God during her evening puja prayer; in summer and in monsoon she would place an umbrella to protect it from sun and rain. Some days she would spend all of her waking hours at that outdoor shrine. This intensity slightly went down after the first *Batsarik Sraddha*, yearly memorial, which was jointly organized by her family and that of Purbasha Satpati of Domjur village of Moulavi Bazar region. Nayan's marriage and coming home of sister-in-law Nalini helped no doubt. As she gained her strength she decided to take a stand in her home of tens of generations. In spite of plea from Nayan, her Sejda, and other relations to move with them, she would only reply 'not until I am unable to take care of my husband, four kids and Purbasha at home.'

Birajbala :

Annapurna, housemaid Urbashi's eldest daughter, who lived with Mishti Mashi in her bedroom, slept in the same bed with her Sweet Grandma, was the first to witness a change in the old lady. Annapurna shared that with her parents who lived in a hut a stone's throw from Mishti Mashi's home. It seems she even gained strength after visiting Mrs. Birajbala Debnath's memorial. Mass murder of poor Hindu Debnath family of Nidarabad village of Nasirpur Police Station of Brahmanbaria-Comilla region took place in 1989, in a relatively quieter time for Hindus. Immediately after the chopped up bodies were recovered, Mishti Mashi sent Ananta and Hridoy with boatman Ishtiaq Ali to find out what is happening to the remains of Birajbala family. After a memorial was built Mishti Mashi went herself this time with Ananta and his wife Monimala, and boatman Ishtiaq to offer her puja prayer at their memorial site. Ananta, Monimala and Ishtiaq all would say, 'there was a discernible change in Barro Ma during our return trip.'

The killings of poor Debnath family appeared in the papers as following:

Memorial of Debnath family : from left Shujohn Chandra (23 months), Shumon (7 years), Shubhas (13), Pranati (13), Niyati (17), Mrs. Birajbala (45) and Mr. Shasanka (70)

On September 24, 1989 Bangladeshi papers ran a story which highlighted the plight of minority Hindus in the Muslim majority land in a relatively 'cordial' era. The story is about a dirt-poor Hindu Mrs. Birajbala Debnath and her family of Nadirabad village of the Harishpur union, sort of parish, of Nasirnagar upazila, sub-

district or police station of Brahmanbaria district of eastern
Bangladesh, barely 30 miles from Hindu-majority Tripura state of
northeast India. Local Muslim thugs wanted to evict her for India,
so that they can take over her small property free of charge. 'No
one pays for Hindu properties' as the saying goes as Bangladesh
still maintains a law called Enemy (renamed Vested) Property Act
through which Hindu properties can be taken over free of charge,
without notice by declaring them 'enemies of state.' But Mrs.
Debnath had no place to go. She held on to the family's ancestral
land of many, many generations. The Bengali daily *Sangbad* of
Dhaka wrote the following story as narrated by a Muslim boatman,
Mr. Abdus Shahid :

*'I had my boat docked at the Nadirabad village. It was in
the middle of the night, around 1 am. All of a sudden I saw a
group of 15 to 20 men force Birajbala and her five children
(into my boat). They were scared to death. They couldn't even
cry. Some had their clothes on, others didn't. Kidnappers asked
me to row the boat. I got scared too. The boat arrived at the
destination Dhopajhuri Bill (riverbank). They had already
brought drums (empty oil barrels), salt and lime. Killers
unloaded them. All of a sudden I saw they were about to cut
Mrs. Birajbala into pieces. Birajbala cried at the pitch of her
voice. She was begging again and again by clutching the legs
of the killers. Killers then cut her into pieces, and stuffed her
into a drum. After that they cut into pieces the eldest dauthter
(Niyati, 17). From distance I watched the younger children
(daughter Pranati, 13, and boys Shubhas 13, Shuman 7, and
Shujohn 23 months old) were begging for thier lives again
and agian; I can't express that in words. Oh Allah! Why did
you bring me here? I was feeling dizzy. The killers buried both
the drums on the river bed and asked me to row the boat.'*

The drums were discovered accidentally few weeks later when

the water level had risen in the river as a school headmaster's boat collided with the drums which floated up from the riverbed. Mrs. Debnath may not have known that her husband was murdered two years earlier for the same reason and his body was dumped in a nearby village well. The family was abducted on September 6, 1989, and tragically each individual was slaughtered, then cut to pieces, starting with the mother followed by the children older in age, so that they could fit into drums while the younger ones had to watch this horrendous savagery.

Inscription: Smriti Samadhi (Memorial) Swargiya (In the Heavens) Birajbala Debnath, Age 45 Years. Abduction September 6, 1989; Recovery September 14, 1989

Body of Mr. Sasanka Debnath, Mrs. Debnath's husband, was never recovered. He was kidnapped earlier, and murdered for not migrating to India. This was the first warning to the poor Hindu families of the area. Mrs. Debnath hoped against hope that her husband will return. No threats against her or enticement to convert to Islam, as is common for hapless Hindu widows, changed her mind. There is a belief among many Muslims that if an infidel can be converted — by any means — then the converter receives *chhowab* blessing from Allah, and reaches a step closer to the heaven.

Mishti Mashi died at peace seeing a grateful Bangla nation has at least built a memorial to the gruesome manner Hindu minorities are being exterminated. Mishti Mashi's younger brother-in-law, Anindya, living 30 miles away in Tripura, India said after visiting Debnath Memorial, 'Such things wont happen in India. We Hindus have no memory. In my state so many Hindus are murdered each year, hardly there is any memorial. In the heart of Bangladeshi-Hindu refugee-run Calcutta, India 20 Hindu monks and nuns have been burned alive at Kashba Bridge in Ballygunj neighborhood few years before Debnath family murder: there is no memorial, no murderer has been arrested yet. When a (Hindu) native of Mrs. Debnath's village, now the Supreme Leader of Indian Communist Party, living in the safety of faraway Hindu Delhi, visited the area to preach Hindu-Muslim cohabitation while choosing not to live with his Muslims neighbors in his Muslim-Majority homeland, local people requested him to visit Debnath Memorial as solidarity against the oppressed. 'What's the point?' The revolutionary replied, 'How can I find time to offer a prayer at Debnath memorial. I don't pray. I am not a Hindu, I am an atheist.' From July 1 though July 3, 2005 another leader, the head of the Bangladeshi-Hindu run Communist-Marxist West Bengal State Government in India, visited a large Hindu-Bengali convention in New York City. He too is a Bangladeshi Hindu but now, as told to a Bengali-American group, but 'now he could not consider his Muslim-majority Bangladesh as his homeland, because he now needs a visa and passport to visit his home.' He was seeking help from Bengali-Americans for 'their West Bengal homeland' all of whom need visa and passport to visit West Bengal, India, and many are not born in West Bengal either? When the group asked for reasons about this hypocrisy, the leader did not explain.

Mishti Mashi returned back with a bit of grass and flower that she offered at the memorial. She confided with her fellow travelers about the true meaning of 'OM tat sat,' You are the Truth, inscribed on top of Mrs. Birajbala Debnath's memorial.

A few years later the leader of the killer gang was found to be serving as an Islamic preacher's assistant at a mosque in the capital city of Dhaka, 130 miles away. A judge condemned him to death. Oldest Debnaths daughter survived as she was married and moved to the Indian state of Tripura. After visiting the memorial the daughter sold the little homestead to a Muslim, not knowing that her family's memorial will survive time. Already a Muslim mosque has been built next to the memorial.

The Attack:

Like other attacks on the village this time too during the evening puja meditation and prayer a warning was served on the family. A severed head of a cow was tossed and anti-infidel venom was spread through the loud speakers of a neighboring mosque. There was no particular reason for this threat, 'just a normal period' people would tell you. Such venoms have become routine, especially after a new Arab extremist-funded *madrassa* Islamic school was established at the local mosque. Call of '*Allah hu Akbar*,' God is Great, sounded to Hindus (non-Muslims) and tolerant Muslims as words less of call for peace but more of blood thirst '*Allah oder hattya karotta*,' God kill them all. Shamsher and his Muslim friend Kadir came running from the mosque with words of caution. 'We're going to stay here,' a poor Muslim protecting an Educated, notable Hindu family! 'This is reality of our land,' Shamsher briefed. 'Rich or poor, educated or illiterate, Hindu life has no guarantee in my land. There are the true lovers of Bangladesh who have stayed with us. Life has been made miserable for our Hindus by those Hindus who choose not to live with us and go to Hindusthan (India) becoming ministers then telling how nice things are here. Why can't they live here? They are worse than our killer Razakars. People like Barro Ma and their family could have fled to Hindu India and be a minister there. Why should they go? This is their land.' The would-be killers had also served a hand written notice asking Dases to close their *toll* school and leave their ancestral property immediately, giving them a deadline for the family to leave their home. Gouranga and Indu, with consultation with other influential natives, decided to ignore. The letter contained some description of their home which was strange because only an individual who has lived at their home would only know that.

On that moon-less darkness many of Mishti Mashi's Own People came after dinner to stay with the family. They didn't want to leave the protection of the family to two students who were staying at the *saamner dalan* entrance structures. Gouranga Das got up in the middle of the night, called each one by their name, and asked his protectors to go home. 'I have experienced these anti-Hindu threats and venoms from mosque loud speakers for the past 50 years. Sometimes even my students who acted as our guardians when they lived among us changed once they became magistrates and ministers. God will protect us,' he told them. Strangely these hapless poor peasants who have no means to protect the family think themselves as protectors yet looked to Gouranga Das as their protector throughout the year.

This time the killer gang was lot more organized with detailed planning. It seems that the call of Muslim *fazr* prayer in pre dawn darkness was the signal for action. In the midst of the blaring loud speaker three men in *lungi* sarong outfit, with faces covered with *gamchha* towel broke open the students' room and immediately tied them up. A second group of two men in half-shirt and long pants, face covered, moved in to block the path between kitchen and the main building, *purono dalan*, Old Structure. The kitchen

struture, *ranna ghor*, contained a dining room which acted as a
sleeping space for maid Urbashi and one or more of her chidren
when they would decide to spend the night there instead of returning
to their hut. The structure had mud wall with tin roof, with a 6 feet
wide veranda, 3 ft high plinth, like other structure to avoid flood
waters. It was separated from the main *purono dalan* living structure
by 3 feet space. A tin cover was added decades ago between the
Kitchen and the main structure to protect members from incessant
monsoon rain. During low intensity flooding, a 12" inch wide
wooden board acted as a bridge between the two structures. As
Urbashi started screaming at the top of her voice, 'Ma, Baba dacoits
are here! Dacoit! Dacoit!' Her son Apurba started screaming as
well. With a kick the killers opened the bamboo door, and silenced
Urbashi with their rifle butt. By that the time the main group had
already moved into the main house first firing indiscriminately in the
sky terrorizing the occupants. They quickly tied up the entire family.
'Didn't we order you not to teach Muslims in your school?' asked
one man, his face still covered. Didn't we ask you to teach 'La
Ilaha Illala,' There is no God but Our God? Why do you still teach
the dirt of your filthy religion?'

Das asked 'What? Are you objecting to 'There is one God
but people address the Supreme Power by different names?' One
of them bayoneted again using anti-Hindu slurs and started
dragging the family outdoors.

Gouranga Das, his hands tied behind his back, profusely
bleeding from the stab wounds, said. 'Isn't that my son
Kalimuddin? You used to enjoy living here. My son, take me
away, but let these kids and my wife go. They have done nothing.
They are innocent.'

The man slapped hard bleeding Das. This was an unbelievable
act in a culture that worships teachers, age and wisdom. This was
the ultimate insult, ultimate dehumanizing like derobing of women

by the Nazis. Urbashi fell on the body of her husband and asked, 'Baba Kalim, don't hit him, take me away. I'll give you everything.' There was no response, but in that darkness a young man probably of her sons' age kicked Mrs. Das, and said, 'Like he said you whore, say in Arabic, There is no God but Our God.' Not knowing what she was saying, Mrs. Das repeated her usual 'There is one God but people address the by different names?'

Mr. Das. barely breathing, spoke like a teacher he was, 'It means, There is no God but One God, not what you are saying, which we believe too.' That was the last word he said.

By this time Das's distant neighbors have already awaken and started screaming 'Help, dacoits are here!' Murderers are here!' The men quickly dragged the family outdoors, and separated Mr. Das from Mrs. Das, and guest student Purbasha, from the children. Killers threw grenades at their wood-cum-mud-cum-tin structure and to the body of the children as they fled. The entire killing took no more than 2 or 3 minutes, like a well rehearsed military drill, but it felt like eternity. Mr. Das's body lay in the front yard with anti-Hindu obscenity scrawled on him. All other bodies were found on a ditch with face down, except for Mrs. Das and Purbasha, who were found inside a nearby shop with clear marks of abuse, their saris covered in blood, left for dead.

As Mrs. Indu Bala AgniBeena Dasi was laid to rest at her own home, next to her family and the tulshi plant, her Own People inscriber in simple Bengali characters, 'OM. There is One God, People Call it by Different Names.'

The entire village sang one of the popular evening prayer songs:

You're our mother, you're our daughter,

You are the child of the Creator.

You're our past, you're our hope,

You'll return to Earth in our Mother's womb.

Chapter 16
Returning Home

In our mobile society 'home' is one's residence, and for immigrants it is also the home of origin; for refugees it is a bit more complicated. In the Indian Subcontinent home is *desh*, which means concurrently ancestral village, region, state and nation. New York is our *desh* for almost all of our school-teacher son Shuvo's and physician daughter Joyeeta's lives, though they were born in Alabama, and left South as babies. Then there is Calcutta, India where I grew up and *Lakhsman-kathi* village in coastal Bangladesh which has been our home since mid-1500s when it was first settled, until the family's eviction following anti-Hindu pogroms after the India/Bengal partition in 1947 when the area came under the rule of Islamic Pakistan [now Bangladesh]. To many locals even *Lakhsman-kathi* is not truly our *desh* home because our family had lived there, for 'only' four hundred-plus years, but it is the village of *Gava* in the same delta region. In *Gava*, it is said that the 'Ghosh Dastidars,' as the family was known through our double last names, had lived from the time immemorial while the written history goes back to 'only' to 10th century. Mother Nature took its toll on the written records prior to that, I guess. Bit-by-bit most of the Ghosh Dastidars and other Hindus fled the area for India, following anti-Hindu pogroms at regular interval.

On one of our vacations we were 'at home' in Calcutta visiting my 90-year old mother and the extended family. Calcutta and its surrounding state of West Bengal is the home to tens of million Bangladeshi Hindu refugee and their descendants, additionally there are small number of Buddhist and Christian refugees as well. At Ma's urging, we decided to visit our Bangladeshi home..Sachi's sister *Mejdi*, the middle older sister, came along hoping that our blue passports might make things easier.

A 20 minute flight, but emotionally eons away, took us to the Bangladeshi capital Dhaka to catch an overnight ship to Barisal City, 140 miles south. Then we traveled 17 miles north in two hours crossing three river ferries to reach Lakshman-kathi. It was a typical Hindu village, which is now mostly-Muslim. At the bus stop we were home again! Everyone seemed to know our home: *Bishnu-Bari*, the house with the 14th century Bishnu (Vishnu) *Mandir* (temple) of the God of Preservation. As we bought offerings for the temple, a big crowd of 'neighbors,' Muslims and Hindus, came forward to take us to 'our home,' this time meaning the building our ancestors lived since 1580s. Our walk along the dirt road was covered with beautiful greenery and pond. Coastal Bengal is really picturesque, especially after monsoon rain when countryside turns green and colouful. Our 'nieghbors' narrated us oral history covering many generations, including the attacks on Hindu families, deaths, injuries, dates, the names of the original Hindu residents and the new Muslim occupiers. A Muslim family who knew our family intimately occupied our home after a pogrom met us with what was unfamiliar friendliness, at the gate across the garden. Our ancestral home is a two story wooden house with tin roof. We were interested to see the rooms where most in our family were born; the *puja* (meditation, offering and shrine) room: the vegetarian kitchen; the entrance tulshi[1] plant prayer pedestal. *Mejdi* was interested to look at the 'women's pond' where our eldest sister, *Didi*, almost drowned when she was three years old. The pond is still there, but not the *tulshi* pedestal, no more sacred to the current residents. A poor Hindu family looks after our Bishnu *Mandir* temple, but the 17th century Kali *Mandir*

---

1. *Tulshi* is a sacred plant in Hinduism. In traditional homes it adorns the entrance. Protection of plant life begins with *tulshi*.

temple, the black Goddess of Strength and Protection, was gone after a pogrom, except for a few bricks at the foundation. Special holy marks on the *puja* room wall painted by women during births, weddings, and deaths — a Hindu custom — are gone, but saplings brought by new brides from their parents' homes to unite with thier new homes, also a Hindu custom, were there as big fruit and flowering-trees. Middle son of the new family, a secular Muslim, requested us to stay at 'our home.'

At Barisal City our host Mr. *Harijan*, from the so-called Hindu oppressed caste — the vast majority of Bangladeshi Hindus, was able to locate the other home village of *Gava*, and introduced us to a *Gava* resident to take us to 'our home.' What was a day-long journey by country boat for our ancestors has now been cut down to a 60 minute taxi ride. In monsoon one has to walk the last mile bare feet through ankle-deep mud, a first-time pleasurable experience for us or a journey by boat taking longer. By the time we reached Gava, word had spread that 'uncle, aunt and cousins are back.' Before 1947 India-Bengal Partition, it was a highly educated, prosperous Hindu village, but most of them have fled to India after successive pogroms. Many of her residents held important jobs throughout India, and with their remittances built schools, colleges, dormitories, roads, libraries, bazaars, ferries, canals, ponds, *ghaat* steps to the rivers and ponds, and bridges. The villagers gave us a tour telling us exact dates and incidents when each of the families fled; the years when the post office, and other institutions closed. They took us around the two ancient land marks: an iron *lohar-pull* bridge over the canal, and the other a shining five-steeple Hindu *Pancha-ratna* (five-jewels) *Mandir* temple, whose deities are gone, and a Muslim mosque has been built on its small property. Next to the 100 year-old high school we were at our first 'home' i.e., at one of four Ghosh Dastidar families who still live there. Fruits and coconut drink were ready. Shuvo was 'just' 19 generations removed, so he was still a 'close' relative. And calculation revealed that he was only 26 generations from an ancestor with the same 'auspicious,' 'goodness' name, Shuvo. Gava and Lakshman-kathi residents kept reminding us, "Remember, this is your *desh*. You are our native peoples." A big crowd was gathering, Hindu and majority Muslim, to see us off at junction of two paths, with a tiny 3'×3' shop selling *pan*, the beetle leaf, and hot tea. Three handsome peasants in their thirties, between 5'-3'' to 5'-6'' tall, all bare-chested in that warm day with folded tight *lungi* sarongs worn like thigh-length shorts joined the group. Two of them were carrying sickles and the third person was carrying a bundle of thick cow ropes hanging from his left shoulder. They walked up from the paddy field 2 to 3 feet below the dirt paths and simply ordered, "Babu, Sir, isn't this your *desh*?" They continued without waiting for my response, "Please tell all these people here that they have no right to change the name *your* Gava-RamChandraPur Union. It is *your* home, and *only you* are allowed to change that. Some of these people have developed allergy of Hindu RamChandra name. You tell them that you oppose this name change proposal." With the rise of Islamization and intolerance, age-old native names are being changed to Islamized Arabic, Persian or Urdu names. To this day I don't know if those friends were Hindu or Muslim.

For our displaced relations we carried back flowers, water and soil from *Gava* and Lakshman-kathi. The warmth of 'our relations' was overwhelming! Still, we were anxious to be back home in America to be with Shefali and Joyeeta, the other half of the family.

Chapter 17

"Keep Hope Alive Day and Night, It'll Happen...."

I like to receive letters and read letters. My luck favors as I return from trips to *desh* home. I receive many letters from my friends and relatives giving me good news. This time too there was no exception. Out of all the letters three letters came form practically the same area, although I received them at different times, but it seems that all of them started writing at the same time, unknowingly they influenced each other's writing.

(1)

Om Ma[1]

Mohammadpur[2]
Daulatpur District

Sneher (Affectionate) Sachi,

Please don't mind for the delay in writing to you. How happy we felt seeing you amidst us is difficult to express, I have told about that to everybody. It would have been nice if you stayed with us a bit longer. After you left us I went back to offer *puja* for you at the same Old Kali-bari[3] where we took you the day of your visit. I am sending a few flowers, petals and *bel* (wood apple) leaves. Save them after touching your head.

You may not know as to how difficult it has been over the past few years. Everything cannot be said openly in presence of others, so we did not tell you everything.

---

1. In the name of Holy Mother; a common invocation among Bengali Hindus.
2. Mohammadpur means neighborhood (pur) of Prophet Mohammad.
3. Temple of the black Goddess Kali, and one of the patron goddesses of Bengal.

12

The small business that your *Pishey*[4] Uncle had were ransacked and looted twice in the last few years. I don't remember if it were five or six times since (1947) Partition. We have appealed to the police, magistrate and to almost everybody else. Last time many Hindu and Muslim boys registered a diary (complaint) with the police and they have told them who were the perpetrators and where they have kept our looted goods. Your *Pishey* Uncle has applied to the Government for compensation. One of our neighborhood boys, a classmate of my son Nantu, who holds a high position was also appealed. He said, "Such things will happen to the Hindus." A few anonymous letters have been delivered in the name of your Pishey Uncle and my Thakurpo[5], brother-in-law. Still we are surviving in the name of *Thakur*, God. In that sorrow your *Pishey* Uncle became practically bedridden. He remained in his *desh* ancestral village home during the last days. When his condition deteriorated we took him to Dhaka. There for quite sometime we stayed at the home of (my son) Santu's friend. How can I explain how good they were? God looks after everything. Still we could not bring him back from there. This is my fate. He broke down after the last *danga* pogrom. He used to say the Bengali proverb, 'Ghost seems to be living among the ghost-busting mustard seeds,' as if the virus is finding home in the antidote. But a man who in 1971 stood so bravely facing guns ponited at him while standing on top of his torched business can't be broken down so easily. He used to say, "As we have ghosts we as well have ghost-busting *ojhas* in our country."

Do you know that our village home has now been taken over by others? When we went to Dhaka with your *Pishey* Uncle we left the house under care of Ghanta's Ma[6], our old maid servant. We also informed our neighbor (Hindu) Ghosh *Kaka* Uncle, the

---

4. Father's sister's husband.
5. Husband's younger brother.
6. Traditionally, out of respect, people do not call others by their first name. Often they call as or Mother of John, Father of Joan, etc.

(Hindu) priest family, and (Muslim) Mannans. Within a few days the (Muslim) western neighbors, Altafs, attacked Ghanta's Ma and confiscated our home. Many of the neighbors went to protest, and a big quarrel took place. Some of them even went to the police. At first police said that your Pishey Uncle and his brother *Thakurpo* Uncle have sold their properties to them. Thereafter they said that it was Enemy Property. At first no one told us about this. After our return, we learned gradually. Ghanta's Ma is with us here. She's a part our family. How can we live without her? *Thakurpo*, my husband's younger brother, has filed a suit. The very next day Altafs slaughtered a cow at our *Tulsi* (plant) pedestral and at our *Thakur-ghar* shrine room, then showed it to all. Does God lose Her respect at this? What do you think? Amid all these difficulties the people like Datta, Bhowmik, Saha, Rahman, Momen, Banidi (older sister Bani), Gomes, Gharami, Biswas and many others of (Unity Council) came from Dhaka, Khulna and Chittagong. I was so happy that I can hardly express, thought it must be *Thakur's,* God's, blessing. I realized that we were not alone. I have heard that Altafs had said something to them. *Thakurpo* said, "Boudi, Sister-in-law, we will have our *grihaprobesh*, house entering ceremony, again on the *Guru Purnima*, full-moon-day".

I gave your gift of sari to my *Chhoto Ja*, husband's younger brother *Thakurpo*'s wife Nandini, after touching the sari at the lotus feet of *Thakur* (deity). It matches her very well. Do I have that age (to wear such a colorful sari)? After that 1955 pogrom, I haven't met *Dada* (eldest brother), *Sejda* (middle elder brother) or Didi (elder sister). When we took your wife to the bazaar and to the *mandir* (temple), we have had lots of discussion, perhaps she might have told you about that. Please ask your wife to write us a letter. Kindly accept our affectionate blessing. You must join us at *Guru Purnima* (full-moon).

Iti (Yours),
Ashirbadika (Blesses)
Choto Pishi (Father's younger sister)

(2)

786[7]

Chandipur[8]
Daulatpur District

Respected Dastidar Saheb,[9]

We have received all of your letters. Photographs of my *Abba*, (father) and *Amma*, (mother), were very nice. My *Mejobhaiya* (middle brother), Sajjad, and *Ranibhabi*, (Rani the sister-in-law), received the gifts sent by you. Ranibhabis must have written to you. They had a great fascination for those. Please don't mind that I could not show you the ancestral home of your (Hindu) friend Arup Ganguli. Even though *Barobhaiya*, my elder brother, agreed my *Amma*, mother, may not have liked the idea of allowing a stranger Hindu entering a Muslim household. I will try when you come next. But, I did't object to that.

That day you told me that I was engaged in anti-Hindu politics. That day I couldn't talk to you. I don't know who told this. You know that *Barrobhai*, elder brother, is engaged in politics, but my politics does not match his. I believe in Islamic politics, and as now the country belongs to Muslims, the nation has to be developed keeping in faith on Allah. Have you seen the condition

---

7. Islamic symbol for God.
8. Village of Lord Chandi, Goddess Kali.
9. *Saheb* is used as a form of address for Muslims foreigners, and elites.

of the Indian Muslims? Our minorities are living the life of the royalty. We have kept them very well, this is what Islam wants.

You must know who have demolished our Hindu temples. Do you know who looted the fish from your washer-man relative's ponds? They are Mohammad Hanif's men. He is now an M.P. (Member of Parliament). What about the Pal's residential home (ancestral homestead)? And Das's land? They are now under the possession of the members of the other party. But they are giving our names. With whom the (Hindu) Naren Gayen's daughter was married off (forcibly)? The *Tablig*, the Islamic conversion, however, was held at our place. This is just a social festival. I selected a bridegroom for the daughter of the poor Dutta (Hindu). It would have been helpful to them. I have heard that someone has arranged for her marriage outside the district. Let them have a good life with Allah's blessing. Do they want to go to India?

I am trying to go to a foreign country. I have entered my name in the lottery (visa) for America. As I have studied at *Madrassa*, Islamic school, I am trying to go to Saudia (Saudi Arabia), Amirati (Emirates) or Maloi (Malaysia). I have heard that Malaysia is also a Muslim country. Have you ever visited that country? One of my friends, Naziruddin, a Muslim, who has passed Intermediate Exam, wants to go to America. I am sending a copy of his passport. If you can find a job for him, please let me know. Please give me your *doa*[10] blessing.

Iti (Yours)
MD (Mohammad) Abbas.

P.S. You can write my name as MD Abbas Biswas, though everybody here knows me as MD Abbas Karim. Nowadays I don't use Biswas (our Bengali family name) any more.

---

10. *Doa*, as Arabic word.

(3)

Om Bhagaban Sahai
(Om God be with us)

Rajarhut
District: Daulatpur[11]

Venerable *Chhotodadu* and *Thakuma*,[12]

Please accept my *Pronam* (obeisance, greetings). Ma and Baba asked me to write to you as they can't read and write. My *Didima* grandma has given me the new sari you gave her. I too really like it very much. You may not know perhaps that my mother died all of a sudden. She had a very high fever.

My *Mamu* maternal uncle of Khulna tried his best. He is the one who has saved my life. Uncle Manjur-*kaka*, of the adjoining village came to take me to give in to marriage to a boy he knows. He brought along a *Maulavi* Islamic priest as well. Since my parents objected to this they beat my mother a lot, because we are *chhotolok*, lowly people, that's why. Now there is nothing left in our house at all. They have taken away everything. Some Hindus, Christians and Muslims from (the cities of) Dhaka, Sylhet and Jessore came to see my parents. They have given some utensils to mother. I have heard that this incident has been written about in their newspapers. Said, they will come again. For quite some time I was hiding at the home of *Mamu* Uncle of Khulna.

He is the one who has arranged my marriage. My husband is studying at Mangalganj College. His *desh* home is Abhoy-kati. He has told me that he will send me for college education. I stood first in mathematics and secured good marks in English and History. (Muslim older sister) Anowara *Apa* has taught me music as well. I have heard that you met her in her school.

---

11. Rajarhut means King's market; Daulatpur - Land of Wealth.
12. Youngest (Chhoto) of Paternal grand-father (*dadu*) and his wife (Thakuma).

Grandpa *Dadu*, please visit us again with brother and sister. Please come to our Abhoy-kati as well. My father-in-law has asked me to ask you to write to him. Would you please send me the pictures of my parents and our house? Please don't mind for writing this to you. When 'He' (husband) will get a leave, he said that his brother and he will repair our house. Please write to him also. We always like to see you all the time. His name is Srijut (Mr.) Sanat Kumar Das. He is in the middle of eight brothers and two sisters. Please give him *ashirbad* blessing so that he could become like Mamu Uncle. Lot of our hopes depend on him.

Dadu, the members of my in-law's family are really very good. They have promised to educate me more. I have no trouble here. I am also sent to learn singing from (older sister) Sandhya-*didi*. Sandhyadidi knows the song that Anwara-didi taught me, and that is a very favorite of my father -in-law. He always asks me to sing that song:

"*Nishidin bharsha raakhish hobei hobay,*

Oray mon hobei habay..................."

"Keep hope alive day and night, it'll happen, for sure

O my mind, it'll happen, for sure....."

Please bless us so that we may remain well at Thakur's (God) *ashirbad* blessing.

Yours,

Srimati (Ms.) Dolarani Das

Chapter 18

Miracles Happen Even Today

This is for true believers, stories of miracles. The proper term is *aghatan* in Bengali, which is associated with divine intervention. In the context of social conditions of our *desh* homeland some of the ordinary events elsewhere become *aghatan* or miracle. These are just such examples. However, if our society were to be peaceful, tolerant and non-turbulent, these miracles wouldn't be worth mentioning at all. The increasing intolerant Islamized society that developed after Partition of India, and then after the independence of Bangladesh, especially after the brutal murder of pro-tolerant *Bangabandhu*[1] Sheikh Mujib and his family, this social transformation, better even, 'social revolution,' is worth mentioning only in that context. With the murder of Skeikh, Mujib, oppression-suppression of non-Muslim minority Hindu infidels took some sort of official form. With them were affected the other Buddhist, Christian, non-Muslim tribal minorities, and tolerant, secular, non-communal, open-minded Muslims. Within the country a large number of Muslim writers, researchers, columnist, poets, and novelists have written about this issue, as have Hindus, Buddhists and Christians. Surprisingly very few 'progressive' Bengalis from West Bengal, India have touched this issue although vast majority of them are of Bangladeshi origin, and they routinely write on similar issues around-the world. But, that needs separate attention. Let me call the miracles Lakshman-kathi and Mahilara, located in one of the remote, but wonderfully picturesque area of Bengal.

In Islamized Bangladesh/Pakistan one form of this oppression-suppression has been attack, destruction, defiling and desecration

---

1. Meaning Friend of Bengal. Mujib was also known as the Father of the Nation.

of Hindu temples, and the other common form has been confiscation of Hindu homes, shops, land, ponds, agricultural farms, and businesses using the Enemy Property Act.[2] As a result many have fled their homes of hundreds of years in the middle of the night, keeping an earthen *pradip* lamp lit as the last witness to their desparate act. Some of them have surfaced in India, but others were lost for ever. A few families have also told me that some have unwillingly changed their names. As one travels the land, one finds that in many cases what some of the ordinary people, unlettered yet wise and secular, have done is truly 'revolutionary' in my mind. Yes, revolutionary of course! Yet, social revolution! These are but two stories from two very ordinary villages. The villagers have used religious symbols, which otherwise, have very little emotional attachment to me.

Both Lakshman-kathi and Mahilara are typical Bengal villages. From a short distance they look like small forests as each homestead is covered with trees: trees that give flower and others bear fruits and vegetables, still others provide shed and breeze. It seems every homestead has one or more of mango, jack fruit, *supari* betel nut, coconut, *tal* palm, *jum* fig, sacred *bel* fool's coconut, *chalta* sour fruit trees and more. There are flowering trees and bushes of *tagar,* magnolia-like *champa, jaba* hibiscus, *hashna hena* and vines of *beli, madhabi lata, jui, aparajita jumka,* etc. As the villages are located in coastal Bengal both are connected with the rest of the world with a network of canals

---

2. The Act was finally repealed on April 7, 2001 after tens of millions of acres of farm land; tens of thousands of homes, businesses, shops, farms, ponds were confiscated from Hindus. Prime Minister Hashina Wazed was the head of the government, and Mrs. Khaleda Zia was the Leader of the Opposition, former and current (2004) Prime Minister who supported the repeal. As of this writing (2005) no property has been returned to the rightful owners, no criminal has been prosecuted and no compensation and reparation has been paid.

built by some of the Hindu *zamindar* land lords hundreds of years ago. Some of the canals have fallen into bad times needing immediate attention and continued dredging. But then again, most of the areas now have good roads, and the need for water-borne transport is now less than essential. Each homestead is separated from each other by bushes, gardens and ponds, but connected with each other through dirt paths. Each home of the poor or wealthy, seems to have one or more ponds, giving away the wealth and status of the home owner.

Lakshman-kathi:

In the past the village had families mostly with Hindu last names of Ghosh, Bosu, Das, Dome, Rai, Datta, Dhali, Dastidar, Gayen, Bhuian, Bhunjamali, Bhattacharya, Nandi, Kundu, Haldar, Sen Verma, Khisa, Sutradhar, Karmakar, Kumar, Hira, Mondal, Tipra and the like. Before Partition it was practically an all-Hindu village as most of the villages are often dominated by one caste, religion, tribe or clan. In the early 1950's anti-Hindu pogrom seemed to have began with regular frequency. At first targets were the educated, and the landed Hindu families. Gradually most of the families evaporated from their native land. The village was especially known in for her 15th century Bishnu (Vishnu) temple. The beautiful 8-feet statue of Lord Bishnu, the Preserver God, is made of black granite. It is said that the statue was found while digging a pond in the village. It is also said that while the virgin land was being first settled as it rose from the riverbed someone had a vision that Lord Bishnu would appear in the area. And it was decided beforehand that Lord Bishnu would go to that village on whose territory it would be found. As a result Lord Bishnu and His *mandir* temple ended up in Lakshman-kathi, and the Lord became a property of the village. Lord Bishnu's eyes were made of silver, and glowed at dark. Now only one of the silver eyes remains as before. From the native elders one hears stories of many graces of Lord Bishnu.

There was a temple of Goddess Kali as well. It is believed to be between 250-300 years old. Between Partition, as the 1947 independence of India and Pakistan is commonly known in Bengal, and many of the early anti-Hindu pogroms in the area, the Kali *Mandir* along with the deity of Ma Kali were destroyed, and Mother Nature took care of the rest of the temple. Now only some of the bricks of the plinth remain as its last testament. Bishnu temple was also facing complete oblivion, only the granite statue remained standing on its own strength. The temple structure was gone. The poor Hindu families had put up a thatch covering called '*mandir*' or temple, to protect the Bishnu statue from the elements. Most of these poor Hindus earn between $10 and $20 per month for a family with three generations, thus falling into the lowest working class of Bangladesh, and the world. After Bengladesh's independence at one of the first visits by one of the expelled natives the local villagers, Hindu and Muslim, requested that the their *Bishnu Thakur*, God Bishnu, deity be taken to India, "otherwise it may ve destroyed by (Muslim) *goondas* (gangs)." They refused. For the last two decades some of the former natives have been visiting their ancestral homeland. In the late 1980s, at the request of local villagers, one of the former residents went back to rebuild a permanent temple structure for Lord Bishnu. With that, glory started to return to the land. Hindu and Muslim *Lakshman-kathians* joined hands to restart a *Baisakhi Mela* fair, which was gone after the 1950 pogroms, in the first month *Baisakh* of the Bengali calendar, in the open area in front of the Bishnu temple. As more of the refugees came to visit their ancestral land, threats on the remainder of the minorities seemed to diminish just a little. It may be worth mentioning that a recent visitor completed his School Final Exam from the local high school which allowed him admission in late 1940s to the Presidency College of Calcutta - said to be then most competitive in the entire Subcontinent, and then on to a British university. He followed his father's footsteps who earlier went to that British university in the 1920s. One of the residents was in the first graduating class of Dhaka University. One expelled resident became the Election Commissioner in independent India. Other residents routinely became doctors, engineers,lawyers, teachers, businessmen,farmers, civil servants in colonial India. Thus although the village was extremely remote, it seems that their standard of education was quite high those days. But as Hindus fled many of the schools closed, as Muslims did not take to secular Bengali or English education to fill up the vacuum.

Lately, care givers to the temples have been coming from every Hindu castes creating another social revolution within the Hindu community. On a recent trip visitors found that the principal *pujari* was a priestess belonging to the traditionally oppressed Hindu caste, but all were quite proud of this fact. Recently, the local Hindus promised to themselves that they will not only stay at the village at all cost, but also rebuild the old Kali temple that was destroyed in the 1950s pogrom. As the old Kali temple site is now occupied by a Muslim family who wouldn't allow the old temple to be rebuilt on the old site, it was decided that the new temple would be rebuilt next to the Bishnu temple. They plan to build a new *tirthasthan* -Hindu pilgrimage center, combining the two temples. A number of Muslims have joined in their effort. In late 1990s two young Muslims became Joint Secretaries of this pilgrimage center project. To some intolerant anti-Hindu individuals and groups these Muslims are 'non-believers,' or *kafir*. Resident Gangadhar Dhali, a poor oppressed-caste individual, said with great excitement, "*Babu*, Sir you won't know how happy we have been the last few years! Even on the days we don't get two square meals, we still don't feel any pain of hunger." On the arrival of 'visiting natives' a smart-looking young man with crisp white shirt and khaki pants came running and said, "*Kaka*, uncle, *Kakima*, aunt, I am Ashraf Jamal (a Muslim). I am a Joint Secretary of the Committee. This is our social project. You are our own people. We definitely want your family with us. We will not take a no for an answer. Please tell other *Lakshman-kathians* about our project." Ashraf is a student at a local college.

"For the last few years we have been organizing the Baisakhi fair. Just like the old days," informed members of the reconstruction committee, illiterate Mrs. Indira Gayen, a Hindu, and college graduate joint secretary Mr. Joy Ishtiaq Ahammadi, a Muslim. Mrs. Parul Bala, Mrs. Ashoka Ghosh, Mr. Krishnapada Bhunjamali, all Hindu belonging to the traditionally oppressed castes, and dirt-poor, and their friends raised their hands and pointed at the area where they plan to build the *tirthasthan*, pilgrimage center.

Some months after a visit by expelled natives, they received a letter from a stranger. He invited them to visit 'their' Lakshman-kathi and wrote about the rebirth of the village. In imperfect Bengali he invited them to join in their upcoming Bengali Era BS1400s *Baishakhi Mela* (fair in the first calendar month of the year, *Baisakh*) :

"With the Grace of *Sri bishnu*

"Ma-Baba, Sir-Madam :

"Please accept my Bengali New Year's best wishes. I don't know if you still remember me, nevertheless I am reminding you. I am one of the servants of the famous patron deity of Sri Sri Bishnu *Mandir* (temple) of Lakshman-kathi village of Bangladesh...........

"........to tell you the truth after the Partition of our land (when there were no more able, educated Hindus here) we still had to carry out the puja of Sri Sri Maha (Great) Bishnu. At present we are receiving vast numbers of devotees. One must see to believe it: the splendid new temple, and the sparkle of almost-living Maha Bishnu. I would request you to visit us in Baisakh. On the 1st of *Baisakh*, Wednesday, at the beginning of the puja of Maha Bishnu, there were large numbers of devotees present. All the respected guests were extremely happy to savor such a joyous occasion. And on the 15th of *Baisakh* Wednesday on the great *akshai-treetiya* (the third day after full-moon) day there will be a big celebration at the Maha Bishnu *Mandir* (temple.)

"Then on the forthcoming Friday the 31st. *Baisakh* at the Maha Bishnu *sankranti* an annual celabration is going to begin for our patron deity Sri Sri Bishnu at the Bishnu temple. We will have *puja, yajna, home* (sacred fire ceremony), *bhog* (blessed food) and feeding of the poor, *anath-seba*. We hope that on that day you will be able to join us and give us the pleasure of your presence.

"Yours truly,

"Sri Naba Gopal"

Mahilara:

Name of the other miracle is Mahilara. Once upon a time there were a large number of families with last names of Sen Gupta, Das Gupta, Datta Gupta, Sen Sharma, Sen and many more of the Hindu *Baidya* (physician) caste. These days it is difficult to find one of their descendants though. A recent visiting group comprised of expelled natives living in India and the U.S., including U.S. -born teenagers. Mahilara was a famous village in pre-partition India. The village high school used to produce many top students in the all-Bengal high school board exam. It was also known for an old *mott* temple built about three hundred years ago on Bengali brick *sikahr-deoul* narrow conical style. It was built by Dayaram Sarkar during the Muslim era of Bengal. It is a brick structure about 100 feet high, and slightly leaning. Thus the temple is also known as Sarkar Deoul (temple) or Helano (leaning) *Mott*. This temple has been attacked many times for destruction, and these days it was being protected by unlettered Rakhal Sadhu or Rakhal the Hermit, and his widowed mother, whom the visitors and locals call *Didi*, Older, Sister. Together they earn barely a few hundred takas a month, between 5 and 10 US dollers. About twenty years ago Rakhal used to wear a long ankle-length *alkhalla* overall made of jute bag. Recently that had come down to a torn rag worn as a *nengti* brief. However, Rakhal's village neighbors have been big supporters of his cause.

During a 1994 tour, some of the visitors thought that the temple was going to disintegrate unless taken care of immediately. Weed was growing everywhere. A few of the *ashttha* weed had grown to 6-8 feet high. Visitors learned that when Rakhal and his friends tried to repair the structure, many of the influential Muslim personalities and those against the preservation of Bangladesh's native heritage opposed it. The reason given was that 'the job is to be done by the government.' Whenever original residents visit the village almost everyone, whether they are well dressed or are wearing only a rag, whether they wear colored sari or the widow's white mournig *thaan* sari, come running to the visitors to share their tales untold since the last visit. After one of those visits, as the natives were about to leave the *mott*, the entire crowd rose to their feet and urged us "Sir, please help us to save our *mott*. If we loose it, our spirit will be gone as well." The visitors asked, "How's it possible to do save it from such a faraway land?" They only said, "You belong to us." The natives conveyed villagers' request to many of the important personalities at Dhaka, the national capital, and in the district headquarters town. And finally they started writing to top bureaucrats and politicians in the government.

Most outsiders when heard about this effort laughed at them. Some of their good friends asked, "Are you getting insane?" But, they just couldn't forget the request of so many 'of their people.' For several years they wrote to the district commissioner, district police superintendent, home minister, minister in charge of archaeological sites, the President and more. Finally in an auspicious moment of June 1996 they were intimated by the Bangladesh Government that their "historic temple would be repaired in the fiscal year of 1996-1997." At first they could not believe their eyes. They read the letter over and over again. Finally they called the letter writer Mr. Kazi about the authenticity of the letter. Incredibly, in early 2000s they got a call from a stranger who was visiting New York telling them how pleased he was with their efforts to rehabilitate the historic place, Bangladesh's heritage. As he told them, he was one of the government secretaries, now retired, who participated in the decision to save the historic structure.

Little over three years ago in another trip as some former natives were entering the dirt path leading to the *mott*, it seemed that a fair must have just ended. Lots of people were heading towards the metaled road. As the visitors went further it seemed that *sankirtan* chanting had ended. Lots of poor Hindus, with some Muslims, from the neighboring villages got together for communal chanting. As Didi, Rakhal's mother, recognized some members who were revisiting she immediately ran towards them with one of her friends. They held them tight and started crying in joy. Rakhal joined them holding other hand so tight that it started to hurt, and said "Ladies and Gentlemen, we all live here and we promise we will live here in the future as well. As they are repairing the *mott* we feel reassured, and we have started regular *sankirtans* again." As they were talking the *kirtaniya* chanting group started singing '*Hori bol, Hori bol*, Take the Lord's name, Take the Lord's name,' over and over again raising their two hands in the typical

Vaishnav style. Two of 'their own people' pulled the guests over and began a dance circling around the visiting natives matching the beat of the Bengali *dhak* drum, *khanjani* cymbals, the metal disc *kasar ghanta* hit with striker, and chanted:

Aachhi heythai, thakbo nischoi;

We have always been here, we'll always be here;

[Our] *desh,* village, *mott,puja,* ritual, fair, *jatra, dol,*[3]

O our Hindu, Muslim, Christian brother-sister

Boley sabey du hath tuley, Hari bol, Hari bol.

Raise your hands; chant one 'n all,

Take the Lord's name, Take the Lord's name.

One of those natives was born in Mahilara. After partition during one of many pogroms her family suddenly ended up in the Medinipur district of West Bengal, bordering Orissa state. Within a short while the native lost her mother, Nihar Kana, a secondary death due to partition. Her oldest sister Didi, then a high school student, had to become the mother of the family. After the passing of another area native in Calcutta in 1999 some of the visitors wrote to illiterate Rakhal Sadhu if a memorial could be built at Mahilara in honor of two departed souls with same name. This is to preserve the memory of the villages which those natives never wanted to leave till the last days. Both of the departed had offered puja at the Mahilara Mott, a famous shrine even in the pre-Partition days. In a prompt reply one *brahmachari* (monk), who rose from the local peasantry to become a *brahmachari*, gave the natives the sad news that "your relative Rakhal Sadhu had passed away at his youth." However the good news is that the Mott has been turned into a communal Sri Sri Nigamananda Saraswat Ashram and Hari Mandir of historic Mahilara Mott ....But after

---

3. *Jatra* is traditional play and *dol* is spring festival of colors.

13

the complete renovation of the temple thousands of visitors and
devotees have been coming to visit us each day. As there is no
bhaktabash or pilgrim-cum-visitor center-cum-school people have
been suffering a lot as they can not return home the same
day.....forcing people to spend nights under the tree" and if they
will be able to present them with a Nihar Kana Bhaktabash School
instead. The natives and their friends at first wondered about the
viability of the project. Once they came to realize its potential and
the need, several families from Bangladesh, New Jersey and New
York joined together to build the center.

A recent letter from the villagers written on 20th August invited
all to attend the Nihar Kana Bhaktabash and School opening in
January and described the foundation laying in that August:

> "....at 2 PM of the past 13th August, at the auspicious
> *mahendra-kshan* hour of the *Jhulan Jatra* (swing)
> festival of Lord Krishna....our ashram President.....laid
> the first brick.

> ".......on the coming 9th January, 7th Poush, on the
> auspicious *Sadhur Purnima* 'full moon day of the hermits'
> the *Bhaktabash* pilgrim center and school will be
> ceremonially opened. You all are welcome with your
> friends and family."

The description of the opening ceremony on the 9th January was
as follows:

> ".......At 11:05 in the morning, at the auspicious nectar
> *amrita* hour, the Committee Members entered the
> Bhaktabash first with the *Shilanarayan*, Stone-
> Representing-the Almighty, along with earthen *prodip*
> lamp, incense, blowing of the conch, *dhak* and *dhol* drum
> beating, ululating and music........

"In the evening three *matua* musician party came for chanting and they chanted '*Hari bol*' Lord's Name all night long so that no one in the nearby villages could sleep. At least a thousand devotees came for *the Bhog* of blessed food."

The villagers told the "foreign" natives that they thought that their mothers, and fathers, had indeed joined with them from the Heaven on January 9 and sang with them:

> *Aachhi heythai, thakbo nischoi;*
>
> We have always been here, we'll always be here;
>
> [Our] *desh, gram* village, *mott, puja,* ritual, fair and *dol,*
>
> O our Hindu, Muslim, Christian brothers-sisters
>
> *Boley sabey du hath tuley, Hari bol, Hari bol.*
>
> Raise your hands, chant one 'n all,
>
> Lord's Name, Lord's, Name.
